Four Strokes of Luck

Four Strokes of Luck

Perumal Murugan

Translated by
Nandini Krishnan

juggernaut

JUGGERNAUT BOOKS
C-I-128, First Floor, Sangam Vihar, Near Holi Chowk,
New Delhi 110080, India

First published by Juggernaut Books 2021

10 9 8 7 6 5 4 3 2 1

P-ISBN: 9789353451516
E-ISBN: 9789353451509

For sale in the Indian Subcontinent only

Typeset in Adobe Caslon Pro by R. Ajith Kumar, Noida

Printed at Thomson Press India Ltd

Contents

1

Bypass Road

The incident occurred on Kumaresan's fifth day at his new part-time job in a shack by the side of the bypass road. The light from the dim bulb encroached meekly into the dark of its surrounds. He had to stay there all night, by himself. If a 'party' made its untimely arrival, he was to call Mechanic Valavan right away, on his mobile phone. This was his brief.

It had all begun like this: one night the previous week, Kumaresan hadn't been able to sleep. He'd lost track of time as he read a novel by the light of the street lamp. Valavan had made his obstreperous entry into the street and braked suddenly by his side.

He'd yelled over the noise his bike emitted, 'What is this, mapillai? You're reading so late into the night, eh?'

He woke most people who had been sleeping on the street before he left.

A couple of days later, Valavan had said, 'You're just faffing about reading books, aren't you? I have an idea. Read your novels in my shack. If you feel sleepy, sleep away. If some party lands up, call me. You'll have some pocket money for your troubles.'

This was how he'd landed the job.

Valavan had erected a wooden frame by the side of the road, hung a tyre from it and fixed a little red electric bulb inside. A makeshift roof had been fashioned from asbestos sheets. Inside this improvised hut were the tools Valavan would need to fix punctures.

Outside the hut was a cot. Valavan had left a little lamp, and one could lie down on the cot and hold a book so that the light fell on the page.

The only disturbance came from the nocturnal insects that clustered around the light. If one were inclined to sleep, one could push the cot away into the surrounding darkness. It took Kumaresan only four days to get used to this routine. He had yet to accustom himself to the noise of the vehicles that zoomed past his post at odd hours. Each vehicle that whooshed into the ether with a screech made him wake up in panic.

He could discern a couple of houses in the

distance. He wasn't afraid to be alone. A book would stave off the boredom. He decided he would read a novel a day.

On that fifth day, the book he'd chosen failed to keep him engrossed. It *was* a novel. But the chapters that narrated the story were punctuated by others in which the author expounded his personal philosophical beliefs. Kumaresan's heart wasn't in it.

Setting it aside, he lay on his back and stared at the sky for a while.

Then, he sat by the road to watch the vehicles.

Then, he put one foot in front of the other and walked along the narrow ridge of the rainwater canal for some distance.

During the intermissions between the passing of vehicles, he felt himself surrounded by a wall of darkness. Some moonlight would have been pleasant. There was nothing of interest at all on the road. It felt strange to walk all alone along the ridge. Eventually, he went back to the cot and lay facedown. The cot with its sagging ropes felt like a cradle. He pushed it into the darkness and fell asleep.

He didn't know what time it was. He woke

with a start when he felt someone touching him.

'Saar, saar,' the darkness called.

The shape of a person loomed over him.

He struggled to sit up.

This was the first 'party' he had encountered at work. The man looked thirty, perhaps thirty-five, years old. He wore unremarkable clothes, a faded shirt and worn trousers, rubber slippers on his feet. But one couldn't draw any conclusions about the people of this area based on their apparel. They were expert at carrying the appearance of penniless paupers while having crores of rupees to their names.

As evidence of his visit to some temple, the party had holy ash and vermilion smeared on his forehead and neck.

His bike had had a puncture on the way home, he explained. He had left it back where it had given way, and walked to the shack. He must have hurried. His face and neck were bathed in sweat. He thought Kumaresan was the mechanic and said, 'Come, let's go.' He was in such haste that he appeared ready to drag him to the spot where the vehicle had stalled.

Kumaresan called Valavan on his mobile. It

rang for a while. He tried twice, to no avail. The party waited impatiently.

'Can we go?' he asked.

'We need a guy,' Kumaresan replied, and indicated a block of stone. 'Sit down.'

Before he could try again, Valavan called him back. As soon as he explained what had happened, Valavan said, 'I'll be there,' and disconnected abruptly.

The party would not sit.

'When will the guy arrive?' he asked, several times, in various ways.

Kumaresan tried to make conversation, but he would not engage. He must be anxious about having left his vehicle unguarded, Kumaresan thought.

Valavan didn't take long. He arrived within the tenth minute of their conversation. The road was a couple of miles from the village. He must have hopped on to his bike even as he disconnected the call. His appearance indicated he'd been interrupted during sex.

He looked at the party, and asked, 'Which bike is it?'

The party gave him the details.

It was of a sturdy, heavy make.

'Where is it?' asked Valavan.

He wasn't able to answer accurately. Not far, he said.

'Which wheel?'

'Back wheel.'

Valavan fetched a broken chair from inside the hut, set it up on the pavement and lowered himself into it.

'Saar, let's go, saar,' pleaded the party.

'Go and do what? Tell me. The back wheel cannot be removed and brought here. There will be no light for me to fix the puncture there. Even if I were to fix it, I cannot fill the tyre with air. Tell me, what can we do, eh?' Valavan asked, laughing.

The party had no answers.

'Saar, tell me what we can do,' he finally said.

Valavan looked at Kumaresan, who was sitting on the cot, and mumbled, 'What shall we do, mapillai?' He made as if he was in deep thought for a while.

'Mama,' Kumaresan began, 'couldn't we take your bike and fetch the wheel?' There must be some way to help the poor man.

'It would be easy if it were the front wheel,'

said Valavan, thoughtfully. 'But we'd kill ourselves trying to remove the back wheel. That's the problem with this particular make. We'll need a proper workshop to do the job.'

'Saar, please do something, saar,' begged the party, coming close to Valavan. 'The vehicle is unguarded.'

'Did you leave it right on the road?' Valavan asked.

'No, saar, I parked it some distance from the road, in the darkness. But I'm worried all the same.'

'Hmmm. I *do* feel sorry for you. What will you do, all by yourself, eh, with that vehicle? Why don't you wheel it slowly and bring it here? I'll fix it.'

'I couldn't push it, saar. It's too far.'

'Well, then there's only one option. We'll have to get a Minidor and load the bike on it. Then we can fix it here.'

'Will we get one at this time of night, saar?'

'Let's see. There's two–three boys in our town who have a Minidor. But they must have drunk themselves to sleep by now. I doubt they'll pick up the phone. Shall we try? But it will cost money. Do you have cash on you?'

'Yes, saar, I can pay. Call them, saar.'

The man's words tumbled over each other. He'd probably sign away all his property just as long as the job was done, Kumaresan surmised. Valavan handed his phone to Kumaresan.

'Call Seelan,' he said.

Kumaresan called. Seelan did not answer.

'Call Santhan,' he said.

Kumaresan called. Santhan did not answer.

He tried four, perhaps five, numbers. No one picked up. Kumaresan began to feel anxious. If only someone would pick up, they could fix the puncture right away.

Mechanic Valavan scratched his beard. 'Hmmm. There's a guy in the next town. He's a good sort. He'll come if I call. But then it will cost some more. Should we try?'

'Please call him, saar. The vehicle is unguarded.' The party came close enough to Valavan to hold his hand.

Valavan took his phone back from Kumaresan, appeared to search for a number and eventually dialled. The man picked up on the second try.

'Chinnava, you home?... Will you bring your vehicle?... There's a party here, one feels sorry for him...yes, I ought not to have called you in the middle of the night, but poor man...come, we'll ask him, no problem...with you, there'll be four of us, and we can lift the bike on to the Minidor... the money won't be a problem, come along...ada! Come for my sake, pa.'

Disconnecting the phone, Valavan grunted. 'He'll land up. If he doesn't turn up when I call him for a job, how will I call him again, eh?'

'Saar, the vehicle is unguarded, all by itself. Please ask him to hurry.'

'Hold on, pa. I've woken up a guy from sleep. He'll have to wash his face-vace, won't he? Come, sit down here.' He snorted. 'Vehicles zoom along this bypass road all the time. But not one will stop. This is an orphaned stretch, don't worry. No one's going to steal your bike. Is it a new bike? Or is this your first time riding a bike? You're in such frenzy?'

Valavan was in a chatty mood. The party sat as if he'd been punished, his head in his hands. He wiped his eyes one after the other. Kumaresan felt sorry for him.

'What happened, anna, are you crying? Don't worry, nothing will happen to your bike. If you want I'll come along. Shall we go and stand guard there? Mama, will you follow us later?' Kumaresan turned to Valavan after trying to comfort the party.

'Who the hell are you, the clown in the koothu? How far are you going to walk? The Minidor will be here any time now, keep your gob shut,' snapped Valavan.

Kumaresan thought: 'Aa haa, this must be the regular stage setting. The party and I are the new characters in the play.' Valavan must have seen many, many panicked parties. He must have fixed many, many punctures in the wee hours. He must have got used to the drama. Once the thought occurred to him, Kumaresan was intrigued about how the rest of the night would play out.

Even before Valavan could complete his next sentence, the lights of the Minidor approached. Chinnavan pulled up by the shack, jumped off the vehicle, and lit a cigarette as he walked.

'Where did this guy come from?' he asked, blowing smoke at Kumaresan.

'Oh, mapillai sleeps here to get parties. He's nuts about books. So I told him to sit here and read, and call me if a party turns up. You know the old proverb about the boy who goes to graze his goat in another village so he can steal a look at a prospective bride for his brother? It's like that,' grinned Valavan.

The party stood up and said, 'Saar, the vehicle is unguarded. Let's go, shall we?' He made for the Minidor.

'Hold on, pa, where's the bike parked, how far? I don't want a song and dance about the money after the job's done,' Chinnavan said.

The party understood that it was all out of his hands.

'A couple of kilometres from here. Perhaps two, two and a half. I'll pay you whatever you ask, the vehicle's unguarded, saar, let's go saar,' he said, flustered.

Stamping out his cigarette, Chinnavan said, 'Look here, I charge five hundred rupees for five kilometres. Then it's hundred rupees for every additional kilometre. Three of us to load the bike, at two hundred a head, so that's six hundred rupees. All right? Do you have the money? Once the job is done, don't whinge about having only so much money. We won't let the bike go. We'll hold on to it right here till you go and fetch any money you owe, all right?'

The party lifted his shirt, reached into the pocket of his trousers, pulled out his wallet and opened the flap under the light from the bulb.

'I'll give you what you ask, saar, let's go, the vehicle is unguarded,' he said. The purse bulged with notes of various colours.

Pleased, Valavan said, 'Right, let's go.' With a smirk, he added, 'You're acting as if you've left your new bride unguarded, not a bike.'

Chinnavan and Valavan sat up front. Kumaresan got into the back with the party. It was open to the sky, with only a low safety door.

'Look here, I'll have to drive for a kilometre before I can make a U-turn,' Chinnavan called. 'So that's one kilometre until the turn and another kilometre to get back to point zero. There's no other way. That's already two kilometres. And if your vehicle's not parked within three kilometres, you'll have to pay according to the rates I quoted. Do you remember where you parked the bike? Did you mark the spot with some reference? I don't want you dithering.'

The party nodded along to everything he said. He must have understood he had little choice.

As they drove through the bypass road at night, the 'sarrrrr' of passing vehicles and their blinding headlights made Kumaresan dizzy. He wasn't sure how familiar the party was with this road. As

Chinnavan had said, the Minidor made a U-turn after a kilometre. When they drove past the shack, Kumaresan said, 'This is where we started.'

The party bent to the window and stared across the road carefully as they sped along. He must have marked the spot. But he did not speak. Suddenly, he called out in a fretful tone, 'Stop! Stop!' Kumaresan spoke into the driver's flap and said, 'Mama, stop.'

The vehicle stopped.

The party jumped out of the Minidor even as it was slowing down, and ran across the street.

'Careful! Watch out!' called Kumaresan.

Vehicles that appeared far away would knock you down in seconds on the highway. The party disappeared into the darkness. He was back within five minutes.

'It's not here, we need to go a bit further,' he said.

'Yov, why do you wake us in the middle of the night and then give us the runaround?' grumbled Valavan. 'Look carefully before you decide. It's already been four kilometres.'

'Drive a bit slower, I'll keep looking,' the man said.

'Yeah, right. If I dawdle on the bypass road, someone will knock us down, understand?' said Chinnavan, speeding up.

The party kept his eyes peeled on the road.

'Anna, do you have some marker? Tell me, I'll look too,' Kumaresan offered to help.

He must have inspired some trust in the man. 'There's a paalai tree, with a little temple under it. You keep hearing the sound of the temple bells. It's to the west.'

Kumaresan knew the road and the town well. But the bypass road had confused everyone. The familiar had turned unfamiliar. Thousands of tamarind trees lining the streets had been felled during the construction. There was only one consistent feature: tar.

Kumaresan closed his eyes and thought hard. The paalai tree, the little temple, the sound of the bells, west, he thought. A picture began to form in his mind.

'Was there a tall fence by it?' he asked.

The party did not seem to have noticed. Even so, Kumaresan was fairly sure he knew where the bike was parked. He considered calling out to Valavan and telling him at once. But then, Valavan might be annoyed and tell him off later. Clearly, they intended to give the party the runaround.

Kumaresan too kept his eyes on the road. When they neared the place he had in mind, he nudged him. 'This is it.'

Then he leaned towards the driver's window and shouted, 'Stop, stop!'

But the vehicle only stopped when he shouted into the flap.

The man ran out into the darkness, jumping over the safety door. He was gone for a while.

'Where the hell did he go?' Chinnavan looked out, irritated.

He returned after five minutes. They had the right place.

'There's no U-turn here,' said Chinnavan. 'I'll have to drive a kilometre at least before I can come round. It's already been over five kilometres. You remember the rate I quoted?'

'I'll stay here. You make the U-turn. I'll wait,' the party said.

But Valavan and Chinnavan didn't trust him. They asked Kumaresan to get down and keep an eye on him. The party ran across the road even as vehicles approached. Kumaresan crossed carefully.

The little temple was in the forest, about fifty feet off the road. Even before Kumaresan had reached the other side of the road, the man had wheeled the vehicle from its hiding spot to the road.

As he had said, the little gongs of the temple bells swung against each other in the breeze. Their musical tinkling carried far in the silence of the night.

The vehicle wasn't new. It must have been bought some years ago. Why had he been in such a panic about someone stealing it, Kumaresan wondered, rather annoyed now. He pulled the bike up to the ridge of the road and sat by it.

As Kumaresan waited, the party hurried back towards the temple and disappeared into the darkness. His fear and anxiety must have given him a stomach upset.

Kumaresan had no idea how long the Minidor would take to arrive. The U-turn was not far off. But Valavan and Chinnavan would stop the vehicle for a while so they could take their time to get here and claim they had travelled a greater distance. Valavan had a workshop in the little town nearby. Kumaresan supposed that fetched him some additional income. He must be paying someone off to be allowed to set up the shack where he had. And the bulb that was perpetually on would cost him something too.

Every vehicle that approached made Kumaresan sit up. Could it be Chinnavan's Minidor? All of a sudden, for some reason, a Goundamani comedy scene came to his mind. In a film, Goundamani takes his wife to a movie. She insists on going to the late show. He has hidden from her that he suffers from night blindness, and decides to wing it. He nearly drives his bike head-on into an approaching lorry. As the driver yells at him, he cries, 'I thought it was two bikes, and I could slip between them.' The memory made Kumaresan laugh. It was somehow comforting to think of himself as a madman, laughing to himself in the witching hour.

Finally, the Minidor did pull up by him. The party had not yet returned. Chinnavan opened the bolts to the back door.

The party emerged from the dark, and began to pull his bike towards the Minidor.

'Look how deserted the road is...what foolishness to ride a bike at *this* time on *this* road...one ought not to be biking down this road even at daytime... What emergency brought you here in the middle of the night?' Valavan kept up a stream of sanctimonious rebuke.

Chinnavan mounted the back of the Minidor. Valavan lifted the front wheel of the bike on to the plank of the door. Chinnavan took hold of the front wheel, while the other three men pushed from behind. The bike was lifted on to the Minidor without fuss.

'Get in,' said Chinnavan, making as if to bolt the door.

'Hold on,' said the party, and ran back towards the temple.

He reappeared, this time accompanied by a woman. She kept her head bent.

'He went on wailing that his vehicle was unguarded, was this the vehicle?' laughed Valavan.

'Is it a new one? You're the mechanic, you should know,' Chinnavan nudged him.

As the couple approached, the woman drew the pallu of her sari around her head to cover her face. She was slightly built. Her brocade sari made her appear fuller. Kumaresan wished he could see her face.

'Yov, what the hell, you picked up a chick?' asked Valavan, angrily.

'No, saar. She's my wife,' he said at once. 'We'd gone to a function. We have some urgent work in the morning. That's why we had to leave as soon as possible. We didn't expect the puncture.' His tone was beseeching.

'Well, all right. But you give us the name of your home town. No, your exact address. We don't want any trouble,' said Chinnavan.

He gave them details of his home town, the names of his relatives and several other identifiers. But there was no way they could verify what he had said, since his town and relatives' towns were all at least ten miles away.

The woman kept her face hidden. It appeared every word he spoke was true. But Valavan and Chinnavan looked askance at him and made a show of not believing him. Could she be *that* sort of woman, Kumaresan wondered. And if she was, would Valavan and Chinnavan strike a bargain with her? If they did, what was he to do?

'Since this bypass came, all sorts of *activities* have been going on,' sighed Chinnavan. 'Can't trust a soul. Well, all right, get her on to the vehicle. And include the *ticket* in your expenses.'

'My wife, saar,' he said, almost in tears.

He gave her his hand to help her into the Minidor. She was so silent Kumaresan could not hear her breathe. She slipped into the shadows behind the man, as if to hide from them. Valavan, who had closed the door and was about to go to the passenger seat up front, suddenly hopped across the low door and joined them in the back.

'What is this, anna, I thought you were going to sit in front, and you've got on to the back?' Chinnavan called.

'I'm tired of riding in front all the time, man,' said Valavan. 'I thought I'd give the back a try.'

The two of them roared with laughter. Kumaresan felt nervous, even scared. He searched his memory for occurrences of such incidents in the books he'd read. He wasn't sure what to do. He wasn't even sure where his allegiances lay.

The vehicle started. The man and his wife stood by the bike. Valavan and Kumaresan were by the left corner of the Minidor. The ride to the workshop would take only five minutes. But Valavan could not keep his mouth shut. He began to say all sorts of things. The gusty night air stole most of his words away, and no one could make them out clearly.

'What did you say, mama? What was that, mama?' Kumaresan kept asking loudly. Yet, he couldn't hear much. But it was clear that he was smirking, that his exchange with Chinnavan was loaded with snide humour.

The Minidor drew up to the workshop. The party held out his hand to his wife. She got down and disappeared behind the vehicle to adjust her sari. The men got the bike out of the Minidor.

'I thought it was a *new* vehicle. Has it been ridden often?' asked Valavan.

'No, saar, it's an old bike. I bought it second-hand a year ago,' the party said obsequiously.

'You were this anxious about a used bike, huh? Once the puncture is fixed, I'll give it a test ride to ascertain the condition,' said Chinnavan, with a strange smile.

Valavan went inside the shack to fetch his tools.

'You get your money and leave,' he said to Chinnavan. 'I'll take care.'

'I'll leave, I'll leave. What's the hurry? Why don't I give the vehicle a test ride before I go, just to see what its condition is, eh?' Chinnavan grinned.

'When have you ever been able to resist riding any vehicle? Even when it's a pain, you do mount it, don't you?' Valavan said, laughing. 'Fine, as you wish. Stay on. Will be good company for me. Mapillai is new, isn't he? Look, his legs have begun to tremble at the very sight of the *vehicle*.'

The man joined his wife behind the Minidor.

'You, come and sit here, pa. Don't you want to see what we're doing to your vehicle?' Valavan called out to him.

They could barely contain their mirth.

Turning to Kumaresan, Chinnavan grinned and said, 'Have you plugged punctures, eh?'

'No, anna, I don't know,' said Kumaresan, determined not to be drawn into the repartee.

'I believe he doesn't know how to plug punctures, da,' said Chinnavan, and Valavan and he laughed till they had tears in their eyes.

Valavan removed the tyre and took out the tube. Feeling it with his hands, he called towards the Minidor, 'Hey, man, the tube's gone.' He added, 'You must have given the vehicle a rough ride.'

The man peeped out from behind the Minidor. 'Fix it somehow, anna,' he said. 'It only has to last till we reach home. I'll see to it in the morning.' There was a tremor in his voice.

'There's no way to fix the tube, man,' Valavan

said. 'You should have stopped where there was a puncture. If you go on riding it after it's given out, the tube goes for a toss.'

'Tell us once and for all. Are you going to be able to fix it?' asked Chinnavan.

'Why don't you give it a feel-up and tell me?' Valavan said.

It struck Kumaresan that there was no word in the language that didn't lend itself to double entendres.

Well, let me tell you up front that what transpired wasn't as Kumaresan expected, and summarize the rest for you. Valavan said they would have to go to the shopkeeper's house, wake him up and buy a new tube to fix the bike. He asked the party to accompany Chinnavan to the shopkeeper's. The man refused. He would not leave his wife's side. So Valavan and Chinnavan went to buy the tube. They fitted the new tube into the wheel.

Quoting the rent for the Minidor, labour charges for mounting and dismounting the bike, the price of the new tube, fees for the mechanic's job and various miscellaneous costs, they asked for an exorbitant sum. The party did not attempt to bargain. He handed over the money and hurried to his bike. The woman, who rode pillion, kept her face hidden all through.

Valavan and Chinnavan, who then engaged in a debate over whether she was really his wife or not, eventually left too. Before leaving, Valavan gave Kumaresan a five-hundred-rupee note. But Kumaresan felt somehow cheated. His heart told him the money had been sinfully obtained. He wondered what he ought to do with it.

Should he give it away to a beggar? He had always believed one shouldn't encourage begging.

Should he donate it to an orphanage? But was it fair to involve another party in the sin?

Perhaps it would be a good deed to put the money in the temple hundi. But he wasn't really a believer.

After giving it much thought, he finally decided to spend the money on a book he had wanted to buy for a long time.

2

Beloved Face

Saraswati pretended not to notice. She deduced from the bits and pieces of conversation she overheard that something about Arvind Swamy had appeared in a weekly magazine. Was it an interview? A pen portrait? A news item? Two of her colleagues were huddled together, reading out a sentence or two, then glancing at her, whispering among themselves and giggling. All her fellow teachers seemed to know her little secrets. She wasn't sure how they'd heard. Gossip chose its own ways to travel. A teacher from this school might have met an old acquaintance of hers at a conference or a training programme.

'Saraswati? She's my friend,' the acquaintance might have begun.

Then, there must have been talk of Arvind Swamy, accompanied by snide laughter.

The exchange would have created a bond between the two, and this shared cattiness would have forged their friendship. No one had spoken to her about it directly. They did enquire, seemingly with great concern, about prospects of her marriage. She would counter their questions with a soft smile.

When films featuring Arvind Swamy played on television, they would discuss it in the staffroom. Their voices would carry from one end of the room to the other.

'They're playing that film with Arvind Swamy and Sridevi in the lead roles. I wanted to take a day off so I could watch it. But I've run out of leave.'

Saraswati would feel irritated. Her colleagues never spoke as loudly while taking lessons for classrooms full of students. But she would stifle her emotions. She'd have to find a way. It would be a long day. They'd keep up this chatter about the film every chance they got.

'That Sridevi...she's gone and starred alongside a younger man! What guts, eh?' one would say. 'Yeah, right, like everyone looks for a suitable match. Some people desire partners who are way out of their league,' another would say pointedly.

Sometimes, they would turn to her and ask, 'They played *Thalapathi* on TV. Did you watch it, Teacher?' She would grit her teeth, but smile and nod.

Yet, they kept up the teasing.

'You should see Arvind Swamy in it. Like a doll made of white flour,' they would say and look at her for a reaction. She would laugh and offer no words.

That day, when her colleagues tossed the weekly on to the table and stood up, she saw his name on the open page. Should she pick it up and see what it said? She refrained. They just may have kept it by her side to observe whether she did pick it up. There had been no news of Arvind Swamy for nearly a decade. His pictures had not been published in the papers recently either. Or perhaps she hadn't noticed, because she'd lost her enthusiasm for collecting them. She'd stopped even buying film magazines. The reason for this might have been her anger at magazines that didn't consistently publish news about Arvind Swamy. What kind of magazines were those anyway?

It had all begun when Saraswati had left her village for the big city to pursue her bachelor's degree at an arts college. She had won a government scholarship. She would be able to study without burdening her parents with the costs. They were small farmers who had struggled to raise their five children on the living they eked out from their meagre holdings. Their four goats and the buffalo calves they raised gave them milk for nourishment. Her father would often boast that he had been born into a heritage of agricultural cultivation. Once she moved to the city, the pathos of his pride became apparent to her.

For a while, the city frightened her. It felt like living in a demon's mouth, fighting not to be swallowed by its greed. Over time, she learned to negotiate the contours of the ugly tongue, the sharp teeth. She could survive. The demon's mouth coughed up odd jobs which would enable her to save money for her expenses, perhaps even enough to send back home. Shops offered part-time jobs. But they wouldn't allow Saraswati to serve customers. There was always work behind the scenes. It seemed fitting that she ought to be put to work where customers would not see her. They did not mind her taking the odd day off. If she didn't like a job, she could easily switch to a different shop. Sometimes she saved enough money to afford a trip back to her village.

The only thing she found unbearable was the harassment from the other girls. Saraswati was dark. And by dark, I mean so dark you'd think she'd worn blackface. Even her mother would sigh every now and again, 'How did you get so dark, like you've been rolled in tar before you were planted in my womb, di?' Everyone in her family was dark. But not as dark as she. She had three younger sisters and a little brother. Her parents, in their anxiety for a male heir, had birthed four girls before they succeeded in having a son.

During their leisure hours, Saraswati became her friends' favourite plaything. It began with the ragging in the hostel.

They made her stand so her body was on display. They asked her to raise an arm. Then, the girls approached her one after the other, pressed their index fingers hard against her midriff, and made a show of applying kohl to their eyes and pottu on their foreheads. Even after fifty girls had helped themselves to her body, its blackness hadn't waned.

They called her 'Karuppazhagi' – Black Beauty. That became her nickname. 'Why on earth did they call you Saraswati? They ought to have called you Parvati,' they would say.

It was a rare day when a girl did not stop Saraswati to poke at Black Beauty's dark skin. Over time, the embarrassment she felt when they touched her faded away. Where once she had squirmed, now she would offer up her face or stick out her hip even before the girl had pressed her raised finger to Saraswati's waist. 'Here, help yourself,' she would call out. Most girls would pinch her stomach for their supply of imaginary kohl. She took to accosting them with her buttocks.

'She's become numb to it all,' they would laugh, to hide their annoyance.

She drew some satisfaction from being a source of mirth to these girls.

'Where'll you find a husband who's suited to this shade of dark, huh?'

'Once he touches you, won't your groom's body turn black too?'

The film *Thalapathi* was running to full houses at the cinemas when the girls in her hostel decided to go watch it. The gang could not stop speaking about the film for days. A crucial object of their discussion was Arvind Swamy, who had made his debut in the film.

One day, Saraswati's roommate Padma said, in a particularly concerned voice, 'Di, if you have a baby as dark as you, what will you do?'

Saraswati wanted to snap, 'I'll raise the baby like my parents raised me.' For some reason, she said instead, 'I'll marry Arvind Swamy, di. Then you'll see how white my babies are.'

Since their trip to the cinema, Arvind Swamy's face had tattooed itself on to her heart. And now her crush was out in the open.

'This sounds like something a woman said to Socrates or Bernard Shaw, no?' Padma laughed. 'What if the babies take after your colour and not his?'

'Arvind Swamy is a burning flare. And a burning flare will engulf everything in its way.' The words tumbled out like self-indulgent poetry.

The sentence spread through the hostel like forest fire.

Some picked angry fights. 'Arvind Swamy is *my* man, di. How dare you have a crush on him?'

'It's all right, we can share him,' others said generously.

But so much was made of Saraswati's crush on Arvind Swamy that she became synonymous with him. The more thought she gave it, the more obsessed she became with the actor. So did her housemates. Instead of teasing her about her colour, they began to tease her about Arvind Swamy. This had given her a measure of peace.

That day, she couldn't bring herself to work. She wondered if she ought to buy the weekly and see what it said. His last release had been *Saasanam*. That film, too, was released nearly a decade after shooting was completed. Was Arvind Swamy going to act in another film? Why? If he had indeed made the decision, it struck her as the wrong one. He could not have. It must be something else. Perhaps it had to do with his business interests. Perhaps he had been invited as chief guest to an event. The change in his appearance would be big news too. People would be keen to read about it. Age did have an effect on appearance, yes. But was he not exempt? Why should he be? Hadn't there been differences in his appearance in *Thalapathi* and in *Bombay*? Indeed there had. But she hadn't noticed because she had been looking at him every day. And because love clouds judgement.

She loved Arvind Swamy with all her heart. She thought of him as a god descended from the heavens to shoo away her problems. She couldn't bring herself to say his name. She began to refer to him as Avar – him. When the film *Roja* came to the cinema, she bought a second ticket for Avar, and reserved a seat for him. She would not let the friends who had accompanied her to the cinema sit on it. It gave her goosebumps to imagine him sitting by her side, watching the film with her. She began to buy an extra ticket on the bus, for Avar. She began to think of Avar as the man who was always by her side. She huddled into a corner of the mattress, setting aside the bulk of the space for Avar. She did not hesitate to accommodate Avar into any activity, to make place for Avar in any aspect of her life. She spoke to Avar about everything under the sun. People would stare when she burst out laughing all of a sudden, or spoke to herself in public places. She didn't care.

He was the most handsome man in the world, he of the flawless round face, its brilliance only enhanced by a little black birthmark. She imagined cupping that face in her palms. Did any other actor have such a perfectly round face? No Tamil actor at least, surely? How did his skin always look so fresh? Did it ever get oily? How beautiful that face was, as if sculpted from ivory! And then there were those deep-set, black eyes, so expressive they spoke volumes even when he was silent. And those rosy lips, which parted to so much promise. Every time his lips parted, a smile crept up his face and made him glow. How could one resist that smile? Had he ever laughed out loud? He didn't have to. One's mouth isn't a loudspeaker, is it? And that *voice*. You could close your eyes and listen to it all day. Its tones caressed you like the notes of a flute carried on the breeze. It could enliven your heart and body and soul. How could one stop thinking about him?

'What is your obsession with him anyway, di? Look at his face, as immobile as a Hanuman statue with a coating of ghee, so you can't see any of its original features!' Uma would say.

'You're just jealous. Acting doesn't have to be all about histrionics. The sadness he conveys with his eyes is palpable. Isn't that enough?' she would retort.

'Di, do you seriously think it is possible to marry Arvind Swamy himself? Everything has a limit, di. Don't ruin your life with impossible dreams,' they would advise.

'Sure, he's married. But I'm happy to marry anyone who looks like him,' she would say.

She maintained a scrapbook with his pictures and cuttings from newspapers. She would look at it and add something or the other to her collection every single day. One of her favourite photographs was from the film *Marupadiyum*. He sat on a sofa, his eyes indicating he was far away from the setting. No picture came close to the dreaminess of that one.

That day, she finished her classes and walked homewards. Home wasn't far from school. She had taken a loan from the bank and bought the house. She could bus it up to the town four miles away and buy the weekly. Should she go home, or take the bus to town? Should she see his face as it appeared now? What could she gain from looking at the effects of age on his face and body? It couldn't be as everyone said. Surely his attractiveness could not have waned? That face had fed her soul for so long. Surely it would last a lifetime? She couldn't arrive at a decision. She didn't want to lose the image she had of him in her mind. Yet, she couldn't contain her anticipation of a new sighting of that beloved face. It was no ordinary face. It was the face that had inspired her to study further. It was the face that had guided her through life, offering her an arm for support.

Her sisters had stopped studying after school. Their parents were hesitant to get the younger daughters married when the eldest was unmarried. But Saraswati insisted she had to finish her education, and escaped the noose. Her sisters were married off one after the other. Before the youngest was married, Saraswati had secured the much-coveted 'government job' – she was to be a schoolteacher. The salary was far higher than one person needed to live; thanks to the pension, she was guaranteed an income for life. She took care of the expenses for her youngest sister's wedding. So that the other two wouldn't feel left out, she made sure she gave them suitable gifts.

Determined to marry her off before their son, her parents found her prospective grooms from across the district. She did look at their photographs. Not one face resembled Arvind Swamy's. Some faces looked shapeless, collapsed into themselves. Others looked long and surly, like horses. Even the structures of these faces were unsatisfactory, let alone the shade of their skin. She dismissed all these prospects.

'We shouldn't have allowed her to study...this is the arrogance that comes with an education. Damned creature tosses everything aside!' grumbled her mother.

Her first posting was far from her village. Her mother offered to live with her. Her father could not leave the village and his goats. Everyone had reconciled themselves to her spinsterhood, and readjusted their interactions with her. They came to her for money. A single woman doesn't need all that money, surely? She never turned them away. She would credit Avar for enabling her to help everyone who needed her. She continued to book two seats everywhere she went. This did pose some problems at work. But back home, she did everything in twos. She set two places for dinner. When her mother was away, it was easy enough. When she came to stay, Saraswati would have to think of a ruse.

'Why does one girl need two plates?' her mother would mutter.

Her mother's overtures persisted like an

annoying drizzle. She kept up talk of marriage. 'There's a prospective groom in this village,' she would say. 'There's another prospect in that one.'

That day, she washed her face and stood in front of the mirror. She was still dark, but the black had lightened to that favoured euphemism for Indian skin – 'wheatish'. Perhaps it was owed to the shelter offered by her teaching job. Other than a slight sense of world-weariness, there was no overt sign of ageing on her face or body. Marriage and children had taken a toll on most women her age. They appeared to stoop under the weight of their decisions. Her face and waist still called out to be pinched for imaginary kohl. She wasn't unattractive. If she asked her mother, the latter would waste no time in finding a groom.

Apparently, Arvind Swamy had begun to go bald. He had put on weight, people said. His face was bloated, and perhaps lined. His hair and moustache and even those gentle eyebrows must have begun to grey. Would he have coloured the white strands? Did he need that gorgeous face any more? What could he stand to gain from maintaining his looks?

Her daydreams had begun to fade. It was hard

for her to conjure him up right next to her all the time. Sometimes, she could not recall his features with accuracy. If this was how it was going to be, what would she do with the rest of her life?

Her mother often said, 'Who'll keep you company once I'm gone, di? Can a woman live alone all her life? Your siblings will come and go. For as long as you pile money into their arms, people will care about you. Once you run dry, so will the visits.'

Had she wasted her best years away? Not all was lost. She could marry someone, an older man perhaps. He would be her husband, her companion for life. The security of her job and her monthly salary had kept her market value high enough. She might even have children. Medical facilities could ensure fertility. It wasn't too late. She would have just one child. A small family. She did not look forty. It was all within reach. It wasn't wrong to desire marriage. The idea of a family of her own did give her some pleasure. All she wanted was a man with a round face. Oh, well, not even that, really. She had become tolerant of shortcomings in just about everything.

She gulped down the tea her mother offered, and made for the door.

'Where to...shall I come along?' her mother asked.

It was her mother's perpetual question, and she asked it every time Saraswati went anywhere other than school. She would accompany her too. It was frustrating. Her mother was yet to cut the umbilical cord. Perhaps Saraswati ought to find another face just so she could be rid of this attachment. This face would offer her a hand to hold for the rest of her days.

'I'll make a quick trip to the shop,' she said and hurried out.

What would she feel if she saw his photograph in the weekly now? The face that she had loved so much over the years could shatter and be replaced by this aged version. The smile could have darkened. The shine could have faded. Perhaps that ought to happen. That is what she needed right now. If she could exorcise the ghost of that beloved face, she would be free to love another. She could live a *real* life with a *real* person. Perhaps the imagined lover who slept by her side would come to life and make her body realize a *real* caress. But to make space for that *real* person, she would have to destroy this image. If she were to see his face in the weekly, that flawless face would melt away. She would mourn its loss for a couple of days. She prepared herself for the pleasure of wallowing. She walked faster.

Before she had reached the bus stop, she saw Waheeda of class 6.

'Aiyo...I've forgotten about the tuition,' she thought.

'Teacher, don't we have tuition today, Teacher?' Waheeda asked.

'We do. You go home and start writing. Teacher will go to the shop and join you after, all right?' Saraswati said.

'Teacher, there's an anna who studies in class 7 in my neighbourhood. They asked me to check whether you would teach him for free too, Teacher,' Waheeda said.

For a moment, Saraswati did not know what to say. Then she said, 'Ask him to come. Ask whoever wants to join in to come along. Teacher won't charge for tuition. Tell them, okay?' She looked at Waheeda's face.

A flawless, perfect face. A round face, like his. A dark face, like hers. She cupped the face in her palms and pinched the plump cheeks. A face within reach. A face that had arrived to guide her through life. A face that had tattooed itself on to her heart. Linking her hands with the hands of the face, Saraswati began to walk homewards.

3

Seemaatti the Buffalo

Everyone woke to the sound of Amma's screams. They had laid out their beds in the open air, under the cool light of the summer moon.

'Amma…Amma…what happened, Amma?' her older son asked, shaking her awake.

She began to sob.

'Your mother is screaming because she's driven herself crazy over the buffalo, da,' his father said with irritation, before sitting on his cot and lighting a bidi.

The older son lifted his mother's face gently. 'Tell me without crying, Amma. Did you have a bad dream?'

The younger son, scared, began to cry too. Amma reached out and held him close to herself. 'Seemaatti the buffalo came and called for me, da.'

'Perfect. If the buffalo calls, it means Yama's calling. Hold on to its tail and go to him along with it,' muttered Appa, gathering up his phlegm and spitting with force. He was angry that his sleep had been ruined in the middle of the night. He found it hard to go back to sleep once he had been disturbed.

'You must have been thinking of the old buffalo. That's why you had a dream like that,' the older boy said, trying to comfort her.

'No, da, she called for me. She called in the same tone she uses when she wants her fodder,' Amma insisted.

It had been a week since they'd sold the old buffalo. The trader had taken her away last Friday. Amma had not been at home then. She had gone towards the forest in the afternoon, saying she had some work, and hadn't returned. Appa had undone the tether and handed the buffalo over to the trader. The next day, Saturday, was the day of the Maniyanur cattle market. The sorrow of sending the buffalo to the market had cast a shadow over Appa's face too. She was a member of their household, part of their family. But what was to be done?

The buffalo had accompanied Amma to her marital home as seeru for the new bride. She had been a year-old calf back then. Little auburn hairs sprouted all along her back. Her stomach alone was swollen like a large urn. She was a good eater. Any fodder would do. She was privy to all the trouble and happiness Amma had seen at this home. Amma would put her arms around the buffalo's neck and speak with affection. 'She's not a buffalo, da. She's the Seemaatti who has come to protect me.'

'What did she give to protect you?' they would tease.

Amma's face would darken. She would avoid conversation with the person who had asked that question for some time, by way of punishment. Once she broke her silence, the force of her words would raise a wind.

'She's the one who's given me her all, everything she has. When she's here, can anyone say I came empty-handed to my marital home? Whether she fed her own little ones milk or not, she's the one who's still feeding my children. She's the reason our holdings have increased. She's been a mother to me, holding me through thick and thin,' Amma would say and break down, overwhelmed. Most of Amma's speeches ended with tears.

'She's blown her nose and wiped her hands on

the walls till they're dripping with phlegm right up to the roof. Heaven knows when she'll come to her senses. Always folded into herself like spathes on a palm tree.'

Amma wouldn't budge at Appa's jibes. 'All I can do to lessen my burden is blow my nose. If only Seemaatti hadn't come with me, would I have stayed here? I would have left you long ago, gone back to my village a grass widow and blown my nose there.'

Seemaatti had ensured the home she had moved into never suffered for want of anything. Just like Amma. Her calves could be weaned within four months of birth, and she would be taken to mate. Even when she was pregnant, she wouldn't kick when she was milked. One could milk her right up to the birth of her calf. When she was into her eighth month, the milk would be so viscous you could hardly get it out. 'Look, it's dripping out like shit. And yet she stands and lets me do this. It appears even Seemaatti has the brains of a buffalo after all!' Amma would scold her affectionately and stop the milking.

The milk, curd, buttermilk and ghee for the house were all supplied by Seemaatti. The family craved these during the three months she couldn't be milked. Once they had got used to the smell of her milk, no other milk seemed good enough. When they went visiting for lunch, Amma would refuse milk and curd. 'A mouth that's used to the taste of Seemaatti's milk would find any other lacking in flavour.'

Of the calves the buffalo had yielded thus far, only three were male. The rest had been heifers. The family would raise all the calves. They would eventually have to sell the cattle for some reason or the other. It had never occurred to anyone to sell Seemaatti. The occupants of the pen were all her descendants. As the clan grew, everyone except Amma had begun to refer to Seemaatti as 'the old buffalo'. Amma had never called her that.

'Like any of you is going to stay young forever,' she would say.

The last time Seemaatti had got pregnant, her suffering had been unbearable. Her large eyes would mist over with the effort of raising herself. She could barely chew the fodder with her blunted teeth. Deprived of nourishment, the calf had been born all skin and bones. Seemaatti couldn't stand up even to feed the calf. Amma had washed her with warm water. She had boiled the fodder to soften it and fed her by hand. 'Don't die on me and leave me an orphan,' she had wept.

By the time Seemaatti had found the strength to stand up and feed the calf, the little one had frothed from hunger. But within four months, Seemaatti had begun to bellow for a mate.

'You're a hag and yet you hear the call of the flesh, huh?' Amma had scolded. She'd decided Seemaatti shouldn't be allowed to get pregnant anymore.

They did not mate her. Seemaatti gave up after bellowing for two or three days. Within seven months, the bellowing began again. Her yield of milk reduced too. Amma did not know what to do. The day Appa said 'Let's sell her off' was the day Amma began to weep.

The two of them would have the same exchange every day for a month. Each evening, the quarrel would begin and end in tears and blows.

'Can we afford to keep the old buffalo here for no reason at all?' Appa would ask.

Amma began to milk her just once a day. Seemaatti would yield a padi of thick milk every morning. Amma would add a padi of water to this. And yet it would taste rich and creamy.

In the end, Appa had sold her to the trader. They did not know whether the buffalo was sold for slaughter or to someone who had use for the daily padi of milk. After her departure, her pen stood empty. Amma would sit under the portia tree in the pen and stare into nothingness. She could barely speak to anyone. She would break into tears all of a sudden. She would wake up screaming as she had done that day, and then sob. It would take hours to console her.

'I heard it, it was our Seemaatti and no one else,' Amma said.

'Go to sleep, Amma. We'll see in the morning,' her older son said and made her lie down on the bed.

'No, da, I heard her,' Amma muttered.

Just as everyone else was surrendering to sleep, Amma woke them up shouting again. 'It's her! I heard it! It's her and no one else!'

She shook away the two sons who tried to hold her back and ran towards the pen.

'This craziness over the buffalo will kill her.' Appa tiredly lit another bidi.

The boys ran behind their mother.

Below the portia tree in the pen, a buffalo was lying down and breathing heavily.

All three stopped in their tracks.

'It's her, she's come back. She won't abandon me!' Amma cried. Having seen them, the buffalo let out a louder bellow. Mother and sons rubbed their eyes and opened them wide. The buffalo remained. It was no illusion. Amma ran and threw her arms around the buffalo's neck. The buffalo licked her. Appa had sauntered down to the pen too. Everyone was shocked. Amma brought as much fodder as she could carry and placed it near Seemaatti. Seemaatti didn't eat. She had grazed somewhere on the way and filled her stomach. She lay back, relaxed, looked at each of them, and bellowed again. The peace of having returned to her rightful place showed in her eyes, which twinkled in the darkness of the deep shadow the portia tree cast in the moonlight.

The ruckus had drawn the people who lived in the nearby forest. It was no ordinary matter that a buffalo several pregnancies old had successfully searched out her home after being sold. Who could have bought her? From how far away had she sniffed her way back? They couldn't stop talking about it.

Ever since she had come here as a calf, the

buffalo had had little opportunity to cross the borders of the village. She may have been to the next village to graze every now and again. She had been taken a couple of villages away to mate. She had been to the veterinary hospital in the city a few times. Other than this, she had only known the pen and the fields in which she grazed.

The Maniyanur market was ten miles away. The trader had hired a Tempo to take her there. Perhaps the people who had bought her lived in the neighbouring village? They hadn't even changed her tether. The rope did not appear to be torn. The buffalo was too weak to have broken loose. They must not have secured the rope well enough when they had tied her.

In the week she had been away, her flesh had begun to cling to her bones. The moonlight betrayed the exhaustion on her face. Her movements gave away the relief she felt upon having finally come home, after enduring the Tempo ride, the market and a new pen.

Amma felt as if a lost treasure had magically returned.

'The buyers will come looking for her,' someone said.

Amma's face fell. She hoped no one would come looking for the buffalo.

No one came in the next ten days. Amma gave Seemaatti silage so she wouldn't have to bite through the feed. She would give the buffalo the most tender parts so her old teeth didn't have much work to do. She sat by the buffalo and rolled the fodder into a ball to place in her mouth, as if Seemaatti were a baby. She made her older son go hunting for a basketful of soft green grass every day. Seemaatti ate the grass. Her health improved slowly. The milk yield, which had reduced to half a padi, increased. The old smell and flavour returned to the house.

Just when they were sure no one would come to reclaim the buffalo, a group of seven or eight people landed up at the pen on the eleventh day.

'Are we going to let you get away with stealing the buffalo from its pen in the middle of the night? The very buffalo you sold? You think we can't gather a group of people to demand justice for ourselves? One ought to kill oneself before resorting to this kind of thievery. We bought this old buffalo because the baby at home needed milk. And now you steal it from us?'

They wouldn't let anyone get a word in. Amma was sobbing, clamping her mouth with the end of her pallu. The buffalo, oblivious to what was happening, stood staring at everyone. The younger son went to keep guard at her side, certain that no one could push him aside and take her by force. The older son was biting his nails from anxiety. Appa was not at home.

Having decided the buffalo had been stolen, the buyers had spent the last ten days scouring the neighbouring villages for her. One of their envoys had spied the buffalo here. Knowing he would be outnumbered, he had gone back to the village and come with a group. One of the men, with a grand moustache and grander mien, was holding forth. He would brook no interruption. The adventure which had begun with the discovery of the theft and culminated in the cornering of the culprits, and the prospect of punishing them, fuelled his speech.

Wiping her eyes, Amma called her older son close and said, 'Your father must have drunk arrack and collapsed somewhere. Wake him up and bring him here.' People from the nearby forests had already begun to gather.

'How dare they break into a house, untie the buffalo and bring it all the way here. Look at the little boy standing before the buffalo. You can see the makings of a thief in him already,' the man said.

It was Raamakka Patti who spoke first.

'Ada! Watch your tongue. Do you know to whom you're speaking like this? This buffalo has been in this pen since she was a little calf. The entire village knows this. What evidence do you have to prove that this is your buffalo? Let's hear it?'

It was only after the old woman spoke that the group stood down.

They explained how they had bought the buffalo from the trader at the Saturday cattle market. They had taken her back this way after the sale, to their village about eight miles further down. The buffalo must have marked the way home. They couldn't bring themselves to believe she had returned on her own. But they couldn't refute the testimony of an entire village.

'Fine, whatever it is. Ask them to untie the buffalo and hand her over. We'll see that she doesn't break free again,' the man said grudgingly.

The younger son moved even closer to the

buffalo, sticking to her side. Amma wiped her eyes with her pallu and stood up. She addressed the crowd in a loud, firm voice:

'The buffalo we sold has returned to her pen of her own accord. She's the Seemaatti we raised. She will never leave my side. I won't chase away someone who has sought me out and waited for me in the pen. I'll give them their money back. Ask them to take it and go. If they want only the buffalo, they'll have to cross me.'

Everyone stared at Amma, speechless.

4

Pork Roast

When Thaathan died, Kumaresan must have been seven or eight years old. It wasn't too hard to make a living in that village, and so his family had lived contentedly in its outskirts for over a year. Their home was a little straw hut by the lakeside, where the birds would chirp and coo and sing all day. They did not hunt water birds for a living. No one from the village ever set traps for the birds. And so Kumaresan could play with them happily. His grandparents, his own family and his uncle's family lived in the hut, making twelve or thirteen people altogether.

Patti had a single errand for the day. She would head to the village every evening. Her only possessions were three pots. On the days the pot she carried into the village was filled to the brim, she would say, 'This is a village ruled by prosperous altruists who fill their cooking pots and not their plates.' On the days it wasn't, she would say, 'This is a village of foraging misers who scrape and lick their plates clean.' She would wake even the children who had fallen asleep and give them a fistful of food. This late dinner usually comprised balls of pearl millet in gravy. She packed the gooey kali in a separate pot. She would soak the leftover millet balls in water. She would squeeze the kali and drink it through the next day, relaxing under the shade of the large neem tree. If she was inclined to, she would trek into the forest to collect firewood or fetch water. She never failed to wash the three pots and leave them to dry in the sun so the smell of food wouldn't linger.

Kumaresan's mother, aunt and the other women and girls of the house would go from forest to forest to gather firewood. They would find plenty of sticks in the organic fences formed by commiphora trees. They would choose sticks that were about the thickness of a finger. Once they had gathered a certain number, they would leave them to dry in the sun. When the sticks had dried just enough to be flexible, they would weave them into baskets. Each time they had five or six baskets ready, they would go into the holdings of the farmers and exchange the baskets for food or money. Sometimes they would go to the markets and sell them. The residents of the village were particularly fond of these baskets, woven from a single unbroken branch. As the branches dried further, the basket would become progressively lighter. These baskets were ideal for gathering cow dung and garbage. They would last a long time. Not even sickles could cut them in half.

The wood stove would be lit only at dusk. The women brought enough income for the family to eat. The men would procure the meat for broth. This job took them all day. At daytime, they would keep watch at the thickets and hollows. During the cropping season, their hunt would extend into the night. A rat or bandicoot or rabbit or monitor lizard would fall prey to them every day. They would trap quails and partridges using nets. There were coconut groves in the village too. Squirrels were prone to climbing these trees and damaging the coconuts. And so the owners of the coconut trees would approach Kumaresan's family to trap the thieves. They would set traps to lure the squirrels. Within a day or two, the number of coconut predators would reduce. Squirrel curry was so tender it oozed the flavour of melting ghee.

Kumaresan got to taste various kinds of meat.

But his days of wandering the forests and hills were cut short by the introduction of the midday meal scheme in schools. He was forced to attend school so that he would have one nutritious meal a day. The teacher had targeted boys like him with great success. The scheme had just been introduced in the state. Kumaresan would go to school on some days, and play truant on others. On the days wheat grains were served, he could not be found anywhere in the vicinity of the school. The school had a single teacher. It was this teacher who had given Kumaresan his name. Since he had been a baby, he had been called 'Eliyaan' because he looked like a rat pup. The teacher never hit him. Whatever the teacher had to say, he would say it with kindness. Hitting the students could drive them away. The enrolment record would be affected. The teacher's kindness was due to this consideration. But the name he had been given was only an 'attendance name'. The teacher would call him, 'Dei, Thomba payale!' – You Thomban boy. Every now and again, he would mock him, saying, 'This guy will eat everything except lizards and chameleons.'

The inhabitants of the village belonged almost exclusively to a community of caste Hindus. The women of this community would neither cook nor eat pork. But one couldn't say the same of the men. They had a weakness for this particular meat. Vellaiyan could not do without pork once in three months.

'There's too much heat in the body,' he would say, or, 'I'm not able to work.' This was a signal that he was going to arrange for a pork roast. Over the next week, he would find ten to fifteen people to share the animal. The advance for one's share of a pig was two rupees. The number of shares would depend on the size of the pig. Once he had enough money for the purchase, he would begin to look for a suitable pig.

The only problem was his wife. 'Shit eater!' she would snap. Or she would say snidely, 'If this shit eater can't have panni, his stomach will swell up.'

He would limit his retort to, 'Will any farmer's wife refer to a muruvaan as a panni?' In that region, pigs were referred to respectfully as 'muruvaan', and Vellaiyan never used the word 'panni', which he deemed pejorative.

He would avoid going home and spend all day

in the forest. He knew every farm that reared pigs in the neighbourhood. He would visit one each day. His visit was timed so he could be at the farms around ten or eleven in the morning. The pigs would have finished their grazing and returned to their sties to rest from the heat of the day.

He would take Kumaresan's grandfather along for company. Everyone in the village called Thaathan 'Poochi'.

'No animal except man will work in this unrelenting heat,' Vellaiyan would tell Poochi. 'You can tell simply by looking at these muruvaan.'

He would select an animal that was neither too young nor too old. He would ask Poochi for his opinion. It was only after he had surveyed at least four farms that he would begin to haggle over the price of the pig. Once a price was agreed upon, he would arrange to pay the money in instalments over a week and hand over an advance. If the price was high, he would try to find more people to share the quarry.

He would tell everyone he ran into, 'You should see the muruvaan. It's like a strapping young goat. Rangan doesn't let his animals go and forage in the muck. They're no shit eaters. He feeds them tapioca gruel. He goes to the town to get them rice, and mixes their grain into tanks upon tanks of water. You should see them gorge on it. It makes you want to join in. It's just the same as raising goats and sheep like we do. Only, they say pork is far better for the body than mutton.'

'Oh come on, do all muruvaan feed on muck? Come to think of it, there are goats that feast on their own shit,' he would say to those who argued.

He was so skilled at counterargument that even those who had never tasted pork were tempted to try it just the once. He always chose Thursday for the roast. That would pose no problems. On Sundays and Wednesdays, most households cooked chicken or mutton. Other farmers might hesitate to forgo that meal and join him. He had chosen Thursday to avert this dilemma.

Once he'd decided on a feast of pork, he couldn't do without Poochi.

Every time, Kumaresan would insist on going along with Thaathan. He would refuse firmly.

'The caste Hindus will hit you,' he would say, to scare the boy.

Once Thaathan returned home, he would smack his lips and speak about how delicious the pork roast had been. Kumaresan thought Thaathan was leaving him out because his portion of the meat would reduce if he had to share it with the boy. The roast must be eaten right there and then. It was an unwritten rule that it could not be packed for home.

Kumaresan longed to go along just once, somehow, even without his grandfather's knowledge. But he tended to sleep with his mouth open until the sun was high, and his grandfather would slip away before daybreak. Kumaresan was resentful of his proclivity for sleep.

This would have occurred on the day of our story too. But he was woken up by a stomach upset.

Vallaayi had said, 'I've heard that the rasam made from the leaves you people pick will taste out of the world. Gather some for me and bring them, won't you?' She had compelled Patti till she had broken tradition to go to various bushes and trees in the forests and fetch bunches of commiphora, spinach and mallow leaves. Patti had brought back the rasam made from the leaves, and Kumaresan had drunk so much of it that his stomach began to churn early in the morning.

Half awake, he stepped outside the hut to go

to the fields, and heard his grandfather saying to someone, 'I'm going for the pig hunt. They'll give me a share. We'll only have two pieces a head. Shall we make broth?'

Kumaresan rushed to the fields, tied his loincloth back on, and ran to catch up with Thaathan. He caught hold of his grandfather's thigh as Thaathan was climbing the bank. Thaathan tried to shake him off, but he wouldn't let go.

'So you won't go back without eating pork. Fine, come along, dammit.'

He hoisted the boy up on his shoulder with one arm. Riding on the shoulder of his tall grandfather, Kumaresan felt like he was flying through the air. Thaathan's loincloth was swinging in the breeze. Thaathan must look like a large black rock moving through the forests. Kumaresan caught hold of his grandfather's head. Once they reached Vellaiyan's farm, Thaathan set him down.

He did not know what time it was. Although they were standing in the open air, it was dark as a cave. The cows were eating in the shed, which had been swept clean of dung. Vellaiyan was tying a veshti around his waist. He was a large man too.

The only difference between his form and that of Thaathan was the veshti. For as long as he was within his own territory, Vellaiyan would wear only a loincloth, which hung down to his knees. But if he had to go out somewhere, he would throw a veshti on over the loincloth and toss a thundu over one shoulder. Thaathan would wear only the loincloth wherever he went.

Once Vellaiyan was ready, Thaathan lifted Kumaresan back on to his shoulder. They would have to walk to the outskirts of the city, where Rangan's farm was. If it hadn't been for the dark and the urgency, Thaathan would have asked him to walk. Vellaiyan was telling Thaathan which of his acquaintances had asked for a portion of the curry. He was cursing some of them.

His neighbour Chellaiyan and he were not on talking terms. It had been a tradition since their grandfathers' times for the two families to take annual turns pruning the branches of the neem tree that stood on the boundary between their lands. The tree had grown enormous and spread its branches over the decades. But even if the branches were to reach the sky, neither family had the right to chop them down. They would pare the tree of its leaves when its shade threatened to affect the cropping fields, cutting them off from the sun. Or the two families could come to an agreement, cut down the tree, and sell it for firewood. The need for this had not arisen. The previous year, while pruning the tree, Chellaiyan had chopped off one of the branches that stretched into the east. Vellaiyan hadn't noticed.

When he had gone to visit the carpenter to get a handle made for his shovel, he'd seen the man sawing the branches of a neem tree. From the frame, it appeared to be a plough.

'It was your neighbour who brought this wood and asked me to make a plough,' the carpenter had said.

Vellaiyan had gone to check the neem tree at once and realized that one of its branches had been hacked. He had confronted Chellaiyan, an argument had ensued and they had come to blows. Chellaiyan had reached for his sickle and spoken threateningly, his teeth clenched and eyes bulging as if he were possessed. But Vellaiyan wouldn't step down either.

Chellaiyan had no shortage of excuses. 'The sickle slipped while pruning and hacked off the branch.' 'There are far more branches on my side of the tree. Don't I have the right to cut one down?'

Vellaiyan would not let go of it. He called a panchayat.

The panchayat's verdict was that Vellaiyan could either cut off a branch of equivalent size or receive ten rupees as compensation for the loss of the branch; in addition, Chellaiyan would have to pay a fine of two rupees to the village's common fund. Vellaiyan did not want a branch for a branch. Even if he were to find a branch that looked exactly like the one that had been cut, a quarrel could begin over who had hacked off more wood. He'd asked for the ten rupees instead. This seemed humiliating to Chellaiyan. But he'd had no option. He couldn't go against the panchayat's verdict. After this, their relationship had deteriorated to such a degree that they hocked and spat when they set eyes on each other.

And this Chellaiyan, who was always spoiling for a fight, had shamelessly asked for a share of the pork roast through Singaan. Vellaiyan had not known this detail earlier. Singaan had paid for two portions, but hadn't specified for whom they were. Vellaiyan had not asked either. He had happened to enquire casually while calculating costs and Singaan had told him.

'How can I let him join?' Vellaiyan had demanded angrily.

'When there's a public event, people *will* join in. Both friends and enemies. We can't stop that, can we?' Singaan had replied.

Vellaiyan was fuming about this to Thaathan. The two of them had been close since Kumaresan's family had first moved to the village. Their bond was sealed with pork. Vellaiyan would join Thaathan on his hunting expeditions at times.

'If it was such a loss of face to hand ten rupees over to his neighbour before the townspeople, where did his pride go now? It's no loss of face to gorge on pork he's arranged to share through a third person, eh?' said Vellaiyan.

'Adhu seri, saami,' Thaathan replied – *That's for sure, sir.* His stock response to most of what Vellaiyan said was 'Adhu seri, saami.' Kumaresan thought perhaps it was mandatory to respond in that manner to the landholders.

'He said he'd cut off one branch because most were within his territory. And now he's able to bring himself to come to my territory to hog pork!' Vellaiyan was ranting when they reached Rangan's place.

The dark of the night had slowly begun to dissipate. Kumaresan slid down from his grandfather's shoulder like a cloth slipping off. The pigs in the sty stirred, nudged into wakefulness either by the sounds of their arrival or by the lightening sky. Rangan was sprawled outside his home. Vellaiyan dug his foot hard into Rangan's side.

'If you drink into the wee hours, like you can tell the difference between the house and the threshold,' he snorted.

Rangan sat up with a start. Vellaiyan's voice alerted him to his surroundings. Once dawn broke, the pigs would set off to graze. It wasn't easy to catch them on the run. Even hens would tire of flying in some time. But pigs could run long distances before they tired. It was the hunters who would have to rest. This was why Vellaiyan had left so early – to catch them before they left the sty.

Thaathan joined Rangan in the sty, which was fenced by a shoulder-high mud wall. Kumaresan stood outside with Vellaiyan.

'When are you going to get trained to catch them, da?' Vellaiyan asked the boy.

Scared, Kumaresan ran behind Thaathan.

'Stay right there!' Thaathan said, chasing him away.

'Dei, make sure you fellows don't pick the wrong pig in the dark!' Vellaiyan shouted.

Just as the pigs knew Rangan's voice, he knew their voices individually. He closed in on the pig Vellaiyan had chosen and stepped on its throat. Thaathan tied the pig's legs together. The other pigs ran to the corners of the sty in a fright. The two men tied the pig's mouth shut and brought it outside the sty.

They placed the pig on a hearse made from wooden planks and secured it with ropes. Rangan would be offended if one called it a hearse. He was holding out a long stick that would help them carry the contraption on their shoulders. He would call the pig's last carriage a palanquin. Every time he saw off a pig, he would say happily, 'My saami is going away on a palanquin.'

In the dappled sunshine of the day, Vellaiyan and Thaathan balanced the palanquin on their shoulders and began to walk. Thaathan had taken the front end, and so Kumaresan ran to keep up with him.

'Stay behind us,' Thaathan snapped.

'Why did you bring this little fellow with you so early in the morning, Poochi?' Vellaiyan asked irritably.

'He wanted a taste of the pork roast, saami. He stayed up all night so I wouldn't leave him behind. You must be kind enough to take this into consideration, saami,' Thaathan said in a pleading tone.

'No one's going to starve from giving a couple of pieces to a little boy, come along,' said Vellaiyan. Kumaresan was thrilled. Every now and again, the pig kicked against the ropes. It struggled to break free. The two men switched shoulders after covering some distance. Kumaresan was running to keep them in sight.

It was bright when they reached Vellaiyan's forest. They went to a clearing with a deep well, which had about enough water for a sparrow to quench its thirst. It was flanked by two dizzyingly tall coconut trees. They were so old they could fall in the wind anytime, and so Vellaiyan had already planted two others to take over from them. The young trees stood dwarfed by their predecessors. An irrigation canal ran from the well to the fields. The water flowing through the canal was enough for the coconut trees to draw and grow.

Five or six coconut fronds were lying around the clearing, drying in the sun. One of the fronds had fallen into the shallow canal. They must have been hacked down the previous night.

Once they had set down the palanquin bearing the pig, Vellaiyan went off to the cowshed. He had some work to do. Thaathan had to finish certain chores before he returned. As soon as he disappeared, Thaathan pulled a surutti from his bag and lit it. Kumaresan was drawn to the tank which had been filled with water. The tank had been hollowed out of a single large stone. Kumaresan went close, wondering how and from where they had carried this stone.

'Dei, don't get too close! If your hand so much as grazes the water, we're done for! They'll chase us out of the village. Come back here,' Thaathan scolded him.

He went and stood by the pig. It was made immobile by the ropes. But it stared at him with its tiny eyes. He pushed a little stick into one of its nostrils. The pig protested and struggled against the ropes. It couldn't make a sound because its mouth was tied shut. Its body was coated in mud. Its tiny tail made rapid, anxious movements. Kumaresan teased it playfully.

'Come here, da,' Thaathan called. 'If the pig pulls hard, the ropes could break. Come and work with me. You won't get your curry unless you work.'

Thaathan was cutting the leaflets from the coconut fronds. He braided the leaflets together. Kumaresan longed to join him in this task. But he wasn't fast enough and kept getting his fingers tangled in his grandfather's as they wove.

Smacking his lips with irritation, his grandfather said, 'Go collect the leaf stalks and whatever dried bits you can find from the palmyra trees.'

The palmyra trees stood some distance away. Kumaresan ran there. Fronds and stalks and leaves lay fallen as if someone had flung them down. The shells from palm fruits which somebody had eaten right under the trees had been thrown carelessly too. Kumaresan ran across the dusty forest floor, dragging the fronds behind him. The morning dew had flattened the dust into the ground, and so it didn't fly behind him. The sound the palm fronds made prompted the pig to jump and try to escape the ropes again. Kumaresan ran back, piled the shells and stalks and leaves on to another frond and dragged it behind him. He christened this the Olaivandi – Frond Vehicle.

By the time Thaathan had finished plaiting the leaflets into thatch, Kumaresan had gathered a great pile of fuelwood.

'Why so much? Go bring the oil to light it,' Thaathan said and began to separate the fronds from the shells and other bits of fuelwood. He could take some of this home and use it for their stove. Kumaresan ran to do his grandfather's bidding. Thaathan lit another surutti.

It was almost noon when Vellaiyan returned. Thaathan hastily put out his surutti and untied the pig from its palanquin. Kumaresan noticed for the first time that the pig was breathing heavily. The animal's stomach rose and fell from the effort. The poor creature's breath would not last long. Kumaresan left his Olaivandi aside and began to observe the pig.

Thaathan took hold of the pig's front legs, and Vellaiyan of the rear legs. They went towards the trees. Thaathan did not release the pig's mouth from the ropes. Instead, he tied extra rope even more tightly around the mouth. Vellaiyan tied the other end of the rope to one of the coconut trees.

In his eagerness, Kumaresan had gone close to them.

'Stand back,' Thaathan snapped. Perhaps he was worried Vellaiyan would tell the boy off if he didn't.

Vellaiyan barely registered Kumaresan's presence. He was preoccupied with Chellaiyan.

'It would be more respectable to eat shit than ask for a share hiding behind a third person,' he said. 'Shameless dog!' He rattled off a list of Chellaiyan's shortcomings as they worked. Thaathan's only response to each rant was, 'Adhu seri, saami.'

They brought a stone from the forest, kept it under the pig's snout and took some measurements. Kumaresan was watching from under a coconut tree. Thaathan set off to fetch a sledgehammer that was leaning against one of the trees. He wondered what his grandfather was going to do. Vellaiyan had climbed over the pig and was holding it down with his legs. Thaathan bent down to the pig's head, which was on the stone, and began to pound it with the sledgehammer. Four or five quick blows, without pause to blink. The pig's struggling movements stilled before the animal could make a sound. Kumaresan had not expected this. He had thought the slaughter would be a slow and torturous one and that the pig would tremble and suffer for a long time from each blow. Perhaps it was better this way, a relatively quick if painful death.

'It's the art of bludgeoning the pig to death that I can't get the hang of, da, Poochi,' Vellaiyan said. 'All right, you prepare it for the feast. I'm going to drink some water and bring the tools.'

Thaathan untied the pig, whose legs suddenly jerked up and went still. This was the final stage of a life slipping away. Kumaresan was still too, staring at the pig, when Thaathan called, 'Come, da, light the fire.'

He ran to the fuelwood and lit the pile from the bottom with a cottony stalk. The dry fronds caught fire and it grew into a blaze. Thaathan brought the pig to the fire, and began to throw the lit fronds on the pig. As the fronds burnt themselves out, Kumaresan brought more along. Watching his grandfather stroke the pig with frond after frond, Kumaresan worried that they hadn't gathered enough fuelwood.

His grandfather called out to him. Thaathan reached for the small knife he kept tucked in his waist string and cut off the pig's ears. He gave one to Kumaresan and ate one himself. The hot, crisp ear was hard for Kumaresan to hold. He tossed it from one hand to the other to cool it. How was Thaathan able to chew it right away, without bothering to so much as blow on it? The ear tasted like a tapioca vadai. Kumaresan was still relishing it when Thaathan cut off the tail and handed it over to him too. It appeared Vellaiyan would not object to this. Perhaps this was Thaathan's share. Contrary to Kumaresan's expectations, the tail wasn't crisp. It felt like soft flesh. Thaathan looked at him and laughed. It struck Kumaresan that his grandfather had had to give up his usual share that day. But Thaathan did not seem to mind.

Thaathan fetched a coconut shell and began to scrape at the pig's skin. Kumaresan went to help.

'Careful, da, it's hot. You do the thigh if you want to,' Thaathan said and began to scrub furiously. He paused at times and felt the skin with his hands. They would have to rid the skin of all the hair. If the men found a single strand of hair in the meat, Thaathan would get an earful.

Kumaresan and his grandfather scrubbed the pig for a long time. If Thaathan felt the skin had lost its heat, he would fetch a lit frond at once, run it over the skin and then resume the scraping. As they scrubbed, the pig's dark coat turned white and began to shine. Finally, Thaathan placed the pig on a frond, sat down to rest and lit another surutti. Kumaresan ran around the clearing and played by himself, chewing on the tail, which had coiled itself up like a bandicoot's.

Not long after, they heard the sound of men's voices. Singaan and Chellaiyan arrived. A large knife with a wooden handle glinted in Chellaiyan's hand.

'So, Poochi, you've finished all your work and sat yourself down, eh?' Singaan remarked.

'All done, saami,' Thaathan said.

He asked Singaan to pour water out for him and washed his hands under it. Kumaresan washed his hands too.

'You're training your grandson to follow in your footsteps, eh?'

Thaathan laughed by way of reply.

'Well, well...thanks to a family of your community settling down in our village, the problem of cleaning the muruvaan has been solved,' Singaan said.

'Poochi's very close to our neighbour, isn't he?' Chellaiyan said in a sly tone, looking at Thaathan.

Even as they were speaking, Vellaiyan entered the clearing with two other men. His face soured as soon as he saw Chellaiyan. He glared at Singaan.

'He said he'd come along to portion out the meat and followed me, what could I do?' Singaan whispered to him.

'We've got enough people to portion out the meat. We don't need any new hands,' Vellaiyan said loudly.

'No one's come here empty-handed. I've paid for it. I've not come begging for two bits of meat,' Chellaiyan said.

'Bring the turmeric, pa, let's start the work.' Singaan brought the snarky exchange to an end.

'Rub it well into the skin to remove the theettu of these people's touch,' someone else said.

The pig had its turmeric bath. Its skin turned yellow. Then they hacked off the legs. They had divided the sharp knives and broad knives among themselves, and each took on a task. As they sliced the flesh of the pig's soft belly, its intestines fell out. Men who were used to this could carry on without flinching. About three litres of blood must have collected in the pig's stomach. The vessel which they had brought to collect the blood was filled to the brim. Two men busied themselves cleaning the intestines while two others sat down to portion out the meat. Vellaiyan asked Thaathan to light the wood stove. Thaathan did as he was told.

The others brought the mutti – the vessel in which the pork was to be cooked – carefully from where it had been placed, by the well. Vellaiyan began to wipe it down. 'Poochi, go and bring the fronds to pack the portions,' he said.

'Get some of the palmyra leaves from my forest too, Poochi,' Chellaiyan added.

They would need the leaves for the roast, but Thaathan did not know what to do. He waited for Vellaiyan to speak. He remained silent. Perhaps he had no objection. Thaathan set off to do their bidding with Kumaresan in tow.

The palmyra leaves, with their serrated edges, rose to a man's height. Thaathan expertly cut out the middle sections alone. Then he went to get the fronds.

'We must make sure the fronds don't break,' he said, handing them over to his grandson.

The fronds, with their leaflets extended like ten fingers, would be handy to tie up the portions into the leaves. Kumaresan held out both his arms for the fronds. The trees from which they picked the leaves were mostly on Vellaiyan's side of the boundary fence. They took some from Chellaiyan's territory just for show. They calculated that they would need about thirty fronds to pack the twenty portions of fresh meat and hold the pork roast.

When they returned to the clearing, the smell of roasting pork had wafted its way through the entire forest. The intestines, blood, legs and pieces of flesh were cooking in the mutti. Some bits of the pig's polished skin and flesh peeked out of the curry.

Vellaiyan was stoking the fire with a palm stalk. Every time Thaathan spoke about eating pork, Kumaresan's mouth would begin to water. Now the smell of the roasting flesh made him drool.

The meat was being portioned out so each person would have a taste of every part of the animal.

'The curry is even more delicious than last time, maamoi!' one man said.

'Look at the skin, it feels like the teat of a cow!' another said.

'The elders were right when they said even a pig is dashing in the prime of its life!' laughed another.

'Has the roast cooked yet?' Chellaiyan asked, making his way to the stove. He put a couple of pieces in his mouth as if to taste. 'Hmm, it needs some more time. And it will have a wonderful flavour if we add more salt.'

'If everyone's going to finish off the roast under the pretext of checking for texture and salt...well, so much for the person who did all the work getting a piece of the meat,' Vellaiyan said.

'Ada, one has to taste before serving, surely,' Chellaiyan said, looking elsewhere.

The two men did not speak directly to each other. They only spoke through snide remarks.

Once the meat had been portioned out, they packed the curry into the leaves. One man would hold the leaf open, while another would ladle the pork inside. Kumaresan was fascinated by the way each pair of hands folded the leaf into a ball. Thaathan handed out frond after frond. Once all of them had kept aside the packets they'd promised to deliver to the others who had asked for a share, the men made for the mutti.

Vellaiyan went some distance into the forest, to where a poru had been erected to keep the sheaves of millet from getting wet in the rain. He returned with two jugs of arrack. The price of the pork included the arrack.

The men took the pot of curry and sat in the shade of the minna tree. It was nearly afternoon. Kumaresan had been starving for so long that his appetite seemed to have tired of gnawing at him and subsided.

Thaathan approached Vellaiyan and said, 'Saami...the little boy is here...'

'What a hurry the Thomban is in, even before we've divided up the curry,' Singaan said.

'If even the men who've come along to portion the meat are in a hurry, shouldn't the person who's carried the muruvaan all the way ask?' said Vellaiyan. He ladled a generous portion of the pork into a cup made from the palm fronds. Then, he gave Thaathan one of the parcels for his share.

From behind Thaathan, Kumaresan's little hands held out another frond cup.

'You want your own plate, eh, boy?' Vellaiyan laughed, and obliged him.

'One is better off belonging to Poochi's

community than ours these days,' sighed Chellaiyan.

'Bring another cup, Poochi,' Vellaiyan said. Thaathan did, and Vellaiyan poured out some arrack for him.

Kumaresan and his grandfather went and sat by the stone on which the pig had been slaughtered. Thaathan drank the arrack. Kumaresan peered at the pork. The blood and intestines had given the roasted meat a black hue. He could make out a couple of green chillies in the cup. He scooped out a mouthful. He had never in his life tasted meat as delicious as the roast. The only seasoning was salt and the green chilli. Afraid that he would finish too fast, Kumaresan chewed his first mouthful for as long as he could. This enhanced the flavour, which seemed to burst in his mouth. Thaathan started eating the curry too.

They were interrupted by sounds of an argument from under the minna tree. It was an old habit for the men of this region to break into fights.

'One man runs helter-skelter to find a muruvaan and bring it here. Another man lands up just for show and demands an equal share. What kind of justice is that?' Vellaiyan was shouting.

'O-ho, justice indeed. You're the great defender of justice for every little thing, are you?' Chellaiyan said. He jumped up swiftly, placed a hand on Vellaiyan's chest and pushed.

'Whatever it is, have your fight after dividing up the pork,' someone said.

'You have the guts to walk into *my* forest and push *me*, do you, da?' Vellaiyan said and got up in a rage. He looked around for a weapon. Chellaiyan beat him to it. He flashed a knife at Vellaiyan.

Thaathan spat out the curry he had put in his mouth, cried, 'Don't, saami!' and ran to throw himself between the two men as Chellaiyan brought the knife down. The others rushed to hold the feuding neighbours back. But no one could match Chellaiyan for speed. He pulled out the knife which had sunk deep into Thaathan's shoulder blade with some effort and leapt towards Vellaiyan, who ran for the forest in terror. As Thaathan tumbled into the canal, only Kumaresan remained to catch him.

5

Four Strokes of Luck

It was by a stroke of luck that Kumaresan got a government job when he was very young, all of twenty. And he was assigned that noblest of professions, teaching. Every time the government changes, the rules governing intake into civil employment change too. Sometimes, the very same government changes these rules. And so, geriatrics nearing retirement age find themselves in government employ at times; at others, youngsters with new blood bubbling through their veins get the opportunity. One must pity middle-aged aspirants. They keep waiting in vain for the rules to change so their lot will be favoured.

Kumaresan had just finished his teachers' training. The rules were in favour of youngsters. He got his certificates as fast as he could and rushed to apply. Before his enthusiasm could abate, he was selected for a job. He was allocated a school through counselling. Several vacancies were hidden to accommodate VIP requests. It wasn't uncommon for appointment orders to be delayed even after employment was confirmed. Some candidates were given appointment orders on the spot. Kumaresan was one of these candidates. Best of all, the job was in his home town.

The Kumaresan of pre-appointment order and the Kumaresan of post-appointment order were not the same person. When he came home with the appointment order, his features distorted themselves into a scowl. He undertook a survey of the house. There were only two rooms. Nothing was in order. He sat down to set everything in order through the day. By evening, he was more or less satisfied with his work. If he applied himself with the same ardour to the task at hand, it would only take another day to set the house straight.

But the next morning, everything was in disarray. Amma had been doing her chores well into the night, only to begin again at dawn. She had been searching for things she needed and putting them back where she saw fit after she was done. This was the reason for the disorder. Kumaresan took Amma to task severely. His rant was an exquisite symphony of pointed fingers, raised hands, ground teeth and harsh words. Amma was frightened into promising that she would put everything back in the order he had assigned by evening.

He saw to it that his shirts were never dirty and that their creases were impeccable. If he could see the lightest line of dirt on the collar of a shirt, he would throw it at his mother's face. He found fault with his younger brother's work irrespective of how carefully the boy scrubbed the shirt. The care he took of his slippers was exceptional. There shouldn't be a single spot of mud on the soles of his slippers when he left home. One could only take four strides before reaching the mud path. But those four strides were of great importance. When he returned home, he would dust and wipe his slippers before entering the house so that not a spot of mud remained on their soles.

He had a single rule for keeping the house tidy: 'Everything must be returned to its place.' Something or the other would change places every day. His eyes alone would spot this. He would begin a grand inquiry to identify the perpetrator. His family cooperated, but no one would own up. He wouldn't let go until someone took responsibility for it. Once, when he was conducting an investigation over who had kept the comb over his books instead of back by the mirror, he snapped, 'Idiots, idiots!'

'It might even have been you who kept it there absent-mindedly,' his brother said. Kumaresan fell silent at once. After a pause, he began to rant about his brother's lippiness and lack of respect. Thankfully, it was nearly time for school and his brother was able to get away.

When he was being served food, not a grain must be allowed to fall outside the plate. If his mother spilt a drop of kuzhambu or rasam while serving the meal, his face would begin to simmer with rage.

'Yeah, yeah, he was Thiruvalluvar in his last birth,' Amma would say when he wasn't around, and everyone else would laugh.

She would long for him to finish his food quickly, get up, and leave. He would not hurry up. He had read in some book that every mouthful should be chewed thoroughly so that the saliva and grains were ground into a paste before they went down the food pipe. This was the only way to ensure easy digestion. And so his jaw would make masticating movements until his food had turned into goop. Only then would he swallow. He did not care about its taste. What could she do about her son sitting and eating for hours? Amma would be fretful until he left the house. Then she would sigh as if a great burden had been lifted off her shoulders and relax.

He had found a job when he was young. The family needed his income. It was no small matter in his little town for someone to be a government employee. So they couldn't complain too much. When he wasn't at home, his father, brother and sister would finish their work. When he returned, no one would be at home. Amma had nowhere to go. She would berate them for leaving her to face his wrath alone. The moment he went into the bathroom, he would shout. Someone had left the soap wet. The empty shampoo sachet had been thrown on the bathroom floor. Nothing was in order. He would shout from the toilet too. He might have spotted a stain on the floor or water dripping from the tap.

Nobody's clothes must get mixed up with anybody else's. Once, when he was hurriedly getting dressed, he put on his brother's underwear by accident. His brother was nearly his height, and so Kumaresan didn't notice the difference immediately. At work, he felt the grip around his hip was tighter than usual. When he took his clothes off in the toilet to check, he realized he had his brother's underwear on. All hell broke loose at home that evening. He demanded why his mother had mixed up their clothes while folding them. He demanded why his brother had not reported that one pair of underwear was missing. There was no discipline at home. Cleanliness came only with discipline. There was no pretence of cleanliness. Responsibility came only with cleanliness. And unless one was responsible...he went on and on for a long time.

When his brother woke up in the middle of the night, he saw Kumaresan talking in his sleep and was frightened by the sight. His voice seemed to echo through the room, delivering a homily on cleanliness. His brother was not able to go back to sleep for a long time. How had Kumaresan not noticed that an extra pair of underwear had made its way into his stack of clothing? Had he not realized when he pulled them on that they weren't his? But how could the boy ask his older brother these questions? Kumaresan had already accused him of being a smart mouth.

The next morning, Kumaresan asked his brother to buy underwear only of a particular brand which he had selected. If they used different brands, their underwear could not get mixed up. His brother did not like the brand one bit. The underwear they manufactured looked like the striped drawstring knickers villagers wore. He had seen a new brand in the market, which made boxers. He had been planning to buy them for some time. Now Kumaresan had dashed his hopes, and the boy began to resent his elder brother.

Kumaresan's sister had been pestering him to put her in the school hostel. The money would be a problem, but staying in the hostel would enforce discipline. The students would have to wake up at a certain time, finish their ablutions before the bell rang, do their homework, study and keep their things safe. If she was taught discipline and order, she would learn cleanliness and responsibility. She would be an exemplary citizen. Wardens and teachers armed with canes would do their rounds of the hostel through the day and night. Students could not get away with disobedience or sloppiness. He told her they would see about it once he arranged for the money. This promise was repeated until she passed out of school. She had no way to escape her brother. The other brother spent the nights at his friends' houses, claiming he had to study for the exams. She wished she had been born a boy.

On a rain holiday, when everyone was home, the others suddenly spotted Kumaresan leaning against the door frame, staring outside. He seemed to be enjoying the sight of the rain. The vision of his happy face, with a smile playing around his lips and his eyes closed as he lost himself in the sound of the raindrops, made his family gawk in disbelief. Just when they thought they were about to witness something miraculous, his face darkened and he said angrily, 'Look at the damned rain!' The pleasant shower had turned into a downpour as the wind picked up speed, and he was angry about this.

His father was in the habit of drinking away the monotony of his job once or twice a month. When Appa came home drunk on one such occasion, Kumaresan happened to answer the door. His father's breath was so laden with alcohol that it nearly got him intoxicated. Recovering, he shut the door on Appa's face and bolted it. When Amma blinked at him, he said, 'A drunk should not be allowed into the house.'

'I allowed my son to study for the wrong job,' wailed Appa, collapsing into a heap outside, his head in his hands. Amma bore this for some time and then opened the door.

'Amma!' Kumaresan said in warning.

'I'm going outside too, da!' Amma said, and closed the door behind herself.

From that day on, whenever her husband wanted to drink, she would make arrangements for him to do it without Kumaresan's knowledge in the kitchen or bathroom and ask him to go to bed quietly when he was done.

But it was hard to find solutions to each of Kumaresan's quibbles.

It was a source of great distress to Kumaresan that the lamp in the kitchen was on even when no one was in there. If Amma didn't have the basic discipline to switch the light off when she left and switch it on when she entered, what had she learnt in all these years? On some days, someone may use the toilet in the middle of the night and leave the light on. The lamp outside the house was left on even after sunrise. Kumaresan would wake up with a jolt on some nights and make sure all the lights had been switched off. If he found that this wasn't the case, he would wake his mother.

'Switch it off yourself, why don't you, da,' his mother would say.

It worried Kumaresan that he couldn't enforce discipline in his own home. For all her carelessness with the electricity, his mother would always switch off the night lamp with its zero watt bulb before going to bed. The entire purpose of the night lamp's invention was for it to burn all night. He would switch it back on. Once, when he turned on the night lamp, he saw his parents in an embrace and switched it off immediately. His mind was deeply troubled for days after the incident. How could his parents behave in this manner when their children were all grown up? Why had he been born into a family with no discipline? They had no discipline in the most basic of things. Where could cleanliness come from in such a case?

He had earned a good name among the teachers in his school. There were only three kinds of teachers – those who enforced discipline very strictly, those who enforced discipline somewhat strictly, and those who enforced discipline. Kumaresan belonged to the first category. The headmaster would seek him out first when any job had to be done. He would finish everything as it should be. He insisted his students walk in line wherever they went. If anyone broke line, it would infuriate him. He would not speak. His cane would do the talking.

One particular incident was to go down in school history as proof of just how perfectly he enforced discipline. During the break, he had escorted a line of students to the toilet and was manning the door. His idea of a line was not simply a queue. If one stood at the front of the line, one should only be able to see the heads of the students. Not even a finger should be visible behind the first boy. One of the boys suddenly stepped aside, raised his hand and said, 'Sir, urgent.' His other hand was holding his shorts. The urgency was not important. But could a whole body move itself outside the line? The moment Kumaresan raised his cane, the body slipped itself back into line in silence. The boy was able to hold it in until his turn came. Kumaresan demanded why he had said it was urgent. Clearly, the boy's sole intention had been to disrupt order. If he had allowed it, the boy would have succeeded. Instead, it had been Kumaresan's success and he recounted this to the other teachers.

A colleague, who enforced discipline somewhat strictly, suggested that he could have changed the order of the line to an extent by calling out, 'Those who need to go urgently come to the front.' Another colleague, who enforced discipline, said he could have told the boy, 'Run to the front of the queue immediately without disturbing anyone else.'

'But what if all the students chorus that they have to go urgently?' Kumaresan asked.

Even teachers with decades of experience could offer no answer.

The headmaster decided that although Kumaresan was young, he was an impressive teacher and his name should be recommended to the government for a Best Teacher Award. They would have to ask their local political representative to recommend his name. Some money had to be spent. He asked Kumaresan whether this was feasible. Kumaresan said they could see about that once the financial situation at home eased. And so the award was delayed.

Kumaresan taught his students a series of 'should nots' – one's handwriting should not be a scrawl; textbooks and notebooks should not be torn; the students' noses should not drip; they should not play in such a manner that their uniforms got dirty during games; they should not make noise. Each batch of students added one more 'should not' to their list – Kumaresan should not be their class teacher that year.

One day, when he had screamed about the clock being five minutes slow and rushed out of the house, his brother and sister turned to their mother in exasperation. She could see the hatred in their eyes. Amma felt this wasn't good for the family, and went up to them. Laughing, she said, 'Your brother has got a boon from the gods,' and went on to tell the story.

Ishwaran and Ishwari were conducting an assessment of all the creatures in the world. 'You do this to fill your stomach,' they would say as each one came forward. The boon they granted was the allocation of a job and livelihood to each subject of their assessment. By the time every life form had come and gone with its boon, Ishwaran was starving. Even the gods tend to get angry when their stomachs are empty. Just as Ishwaran and Ishwari were leaving to eat, a louse came running. It had overslept. Ishwaran and Ishwari did not notice. The louse fell at Ishwaran's feet and begged, 'Please, saami, tell me where I should go live.' 'Go live in someone's hair!' Ishwaran said angrily. Once he had given an order, not even he could rescind it. The louse went away in tears to live in someone's hair. The sight of its tears and the sound of its wails troubled Ishwaran and Ishwari. If only they had held back their anger for a moment, they would not have condemned one creature to a miserable life. Or, if only that creature had had the discipline to sleep and wake up at the right time, it could have avoided this fate, they thought.

Just then, Kumaresan walked in. 'I was born the first son of a family in penury, so it took me some time to finish all my work and come here,' he said. Ishwaran and Ishwari, humbled by their poor handling of the louse, said, 'Fine, go enforce discipline in all things,' and sent him to earth with that boon. That's why he had got a teacher's job,

Amma said. Her younger children were familiar with the first half of the story, but liked the ending of her version very much. It cheered them up immensely to think of Kumaresan receiving a boon thanks to arriving later than a louse.

That evening, Kumaresan entered the house when his sister was lying on the straw mat and reading her notes.

'Chhi! What kind of habit is this, to study while lying down?' he raged.

His sister sat up at once. She felt everything she had just learnt had gone right out of her head. Her face began to crumple. Her other brother saw this and whispered in her ear, 'Boon.' She began to laugh at once. They started dealing with their brother's anger by whispering 'boon' to each other.

'He arrived later than a louse, don't we know?' they would laugh when he wasn't around. And so the story of Kumaresan getting a boon from the gods began to spread. After all, the point of a story is to give one the tools to handle a situation. The whispers made their way to Kumaresan's ears. He consoled himself saying he had got a boon from the gods after all: that was nothing to be ashamed of. The story grew arms and legs. Kumaresan had held on to Ishwaran's and Ishwari's feet and sobbed. When he had entered their abode, his nose was dripping and the phlegm had reached his mouth. When he had left after getting the boon, he had noticed that the windows of Kailash were slamming against their frames in the wind. He had fastened the windows and bolted the doors, surprising Ishwaran and Ishwari with his discipline.

Once, his father said Ishwari had wiped his nose and washed his feet before sending him on his way. 'Ishwari herself has washed the feet of my son,' he would slur in his drunken stupor.

Now that he had to act in accordance with a divine boon, Kumaresan felt compelled to enforce discipline with more rigour than before. This became apparent when they tried to find him a bride. Amma was keen to get him married off as soon as possible. She was determined to send him and his wife to their own house as soon as they were married. But finding a wife was no easy task. In their caste, it was the rare woman who was educated. And the rarest of rare who was employed on merit of her education. Kumaresan thought at first that his wife should be a teacher.

Teachers would be naturally disciplined, and she would raise their children with discipline too. Once it was clear that this would be impossible, he reconciled himself to marrying a woman with an average education. They went to look at several prospective brides. He did not like any of them. He did not give much importance to beauty. But his wife must behave with discipline and propriety.

One prospective bride wore a blouse of which one sleeve was longer than the other. 'The tailor would have stitched it in a hurry. So what, da?' Amma said. But how could he live with a woman whose blouse lacked discipline? Another girl had let her hair fall over her forehead. Shouldn't she have combed her hair properly?

'These days, it's a style to wear one's hair over the forehead like that, da,' Amma said. But Kumaresan was having none of it.

The pottu was not proper; the sari was not proper; the girl did not know how to wear her jewellery properly; the girl did not take away the coffee tumblers properly; the marudhaani on her hands had not been applied properly. He rejected several brides over their lack of propriety. It did not appear he would get married in this lifetime,

Amma thought worriedly. She got into the habit of going into each prospective bride's bedroom before Kumaresan saw the girl, and setting everything in order on her person. But he would always find some fault.

In some houses, the girls were critical of a mother-in-law who was already telling them how to wear their clothes.

'What a boon this fellow has got!' Amma thought in despair.

Since they had started looking for a bride, he was so focused on the flaws of the women that he had forgotten about the flaws of the house. This provided some respite to everyone.

'Ask him to find a girl himself,' Appa said in irritation.

'You think he's capable of that? Which girl who knows him would agree to marry him?' Amma said.

They were not able to find a solution to the problem. None of their friends or relatives had useful suggestions either. The search continued. Many families were keen to get their daughters married to a schoolteacher. He would not have excessive work. He would have lots of holidays.

The salary was good. A teacher had social capital. One of the reasons for teachers to be held in such high esteem was that the local newspapers carried reports on scams worth several crores in tiny boxes, while the headlines in enormous print would scream 'Jackpot for Teachers!' and 'Lucky Prize for Teachers!' every time the government increased teachers' salaries by so much as one per cent.

Even as he rejected bride after bride, others stepped forward to offer their daughters in marriage. The father of one girl whom he had rejected back when they had first begun to look for a bride persisted in various ways. She had studied up to class 5. She was dark. The father decided Kumaresan had rejected her because of her colour and offered more money and jewellery as dowry. Kumaresan's family had forgotten why he had rejected the girl. Then they remembered that it was because her nails were black from dirt. His problem was not the colour of her skin, but the colour of her nails.

'If she can't even cut her nails and keep them clean, how can we expect her to keep anything clean, Amma?' Kumaresan said.

'Aiyo, is the girl a teacher like you? She does

work around the house! Can anyone do household work without getting their nails dirty? We have to wash vessels, sweep the house, scrub the clothes... here, look at my nails, they're black too. Even if I cut them, they look dirty. Women can't cut the nails of their thumbs. We need those nails to peel onions, snip off the ends of chillies...' Amma explained patiently. He couldn't fault her reasoning.

'You'll come up with an explanation for everything,' he grumbled.

'Once you marry her and bring her home, we'll see that her nails are clean. I'll peel the onions for her,' Amma said with a straight face. He was silent.

He had tired of looking for a bride too. He was also worried because his body seemed to have grown less disciplined – the release into his lungi, which used to happen once a week, now happened every other day. Perhaps he was letting go of propriety too. His mother took his silence for consent and told the girl's family. Just as he had got a job at twenty by a stroke of luck, he was married at twenty-five.

To tell the truth, his wife was like his job – pressure-free. One might even say she was less trouble. He needed a cane in school. He didn't need anything at home to keep order. He used a series of verbs on her – come, go, give, put, keep, sleep, lie down, remove, pour. The verbs he used most often in school were: stand, sit, write, study, run. When he told her off for being sloppy about some task, she would hear him out in silence. 'Don't repeat this,' he would sign off. 'Seringa,' she would say – all right. The students said, 'Seringa, sir.' His wife had had a million chores at home before marriage. Handling Kumaresan was far easier.

When the couple left the family's house for a new home of their own, his mother had given her a series of instructions about keeping her nails clean. She did her best. It would be hard to peel pearl onions. But if they used regular onions, she could skin them with a knife. They had accumulated plastic bags from buying groceries. She used these bags over her hands like gloves, securing them with rubber bands, and went about her chores. This worked well. Kumaresan's eyes would wander to her fingers at least once a day. Her fastidious maintenance of her nails pleased him. She didn't touch his things without permission. If he happened to find something out of place despite her careful adherence to his system, he would recite his old rule: 'Everything must be returned to its place.' Although it hadn't been written down, the walls of the house seemed to broadcast the line.

The days on which he delivered particularly long lectures on order, discipline, cleanliness and responsibility saw her go to her in-laws' home and cry. Amma would laugh and say, 'That's how he is.' She was relieved she had made her escape. His brother would say, 'Boon.' 'Anni, the exams are going on in his school now. He only has you to deliver his lectures to for now. Once school reopens, everything will be all right,' his sister would say. His wife would return home, comforted by their words.

One night about two months into their marriage, Kumaresan's face was buried in her neck when he suddenly jerked his head up and asked, 'Did you bathe?' She stared at him in shock. 'Go bathe and come,' he said, and moved away. She did not get up. Her humiliation poured out in tears. After some time, he turned to her and said, 'Sorry...sorry...I should cut off my nose and throw it away.' After this incident, she began to bathe twice a day – once in the morning and once at night. She was terrified she would hear those words again. And then he had another stroke of luck.

In the third month of their marriage, his wife had her first bout of morning sickness. He left her at her parents' place for the birth of the child. He tried living alone for a week. As usual, he would spot a lack of order every time he returned. But whom could he shout at? He wasn't able to get through the day without telling someone off. He went to his mother's house in the next street. It would be seven or eight months before his wife had her baby. They wouldn't send her back with a newborn child. The baby would be seven or eight months old before his wife returned. So he would be alone for over a year.

Amma was scared he would decide to move in with them until his wife returned. Appa bemoaned the impending loss of their peace, after only three months. It was Kumaresan's siblings who gave his mother an idea. The house should not be left unguarded. Let Kumaresan stay there. They would take him food from Amma's house. Brother and sister, who fussed over the smallest errand Amma asked them to run, never missed their turns taking the food to Kumaresan and bringing back the empty containers. They tried not to let him see them when they came and went.

Kumaresan visited his wife at her parents' a couple of times. She looked after him well enough. But there was no order in that house. He didn't like it one bit. He didn't have the freedom to complain about it either. He couldn't even tell his wife off before her parents.

Just as he was getting frustrated with the situation, his neighbour paid him a visit. The man said his son was always playing outside and didn't study properly. Would he consider giving the boy private tuition? He had heard that Kumaresan was a teacher who enforced discipline very strictly and would set any student straight, however sloppy the boy was. Kumaresan began his tuition classes with great joy.

The neighbour was not in a club of one. There were scores of parents who were anxious about their children's lack of discipline. They crowded his home, asking him to take classes for their sons. His evenings were spent in bliss. Which student is ever disciplined? Just as in school, he had a lot to fault with his students during tuition too. It was hard enough to get students to sit still for an hour. He had the grand responsibility of disciplining boys who pinched and poked and punched each other. For a year and a half, he had this wonderful job with the additional benefit of extra income.

He had always been lucky. He had been born with a boon from the gods. His wife returned with a beautiful daughter, who had just begun to crawl on all fours. He named the child Ridishna. An astrologer had told him the child's name must begin with the syllable 'ri'. He had suggested names like Rishka, Riksha, Rimba, Ridha, Riththa, Rithina, Ringa, Richika, Ridiksha, Ridishna and others. Kumaresan had chosen Ridishna. He had asked a Tamil teacher in his school if this was a good name.

'Oh yes,' the Tamil teacher had said and had begun to dissect the name. 'Ridi' sounded like 'rhythm'. 'Rhythm' was the English translation of the Tamil word 'sandam'. What was sandam? It was sound with inherent discipline, sound that followed patterns. Therefore, 'Ridishna' meant 'a girl with discipline', or 'a personification of rhythm'

– 'a girl who embodies sound with inherent discipline'. This explanation was appealing to Kumaresan. But he had another doubt. Was it a Tamil name? If it was a Tamil name, he could tell people about this with pride. The Tamil teacher did love his language, but he also tended to follow the mainstream. 'The first language spoken in the world was Tamil. Every other language has its roots in Tamil. And therefore every word is really a Tamil word,' he told Kumaresan.

Ridishna did not have the discipline her name suggested. She fussed constantly. One couldn't keep anything within her reach. She would tug at it till it fell to the floor. Or she would put it in her mouth. She would throw it with all her force until it broke. The joy of watching the child lasted a couple of days. Once, when he was cooing to her, she pooped on his lap. When he was eating, she pooped right next to his plate. She reached for a book and shred it to pieces before his eyes. It was the class 1 textbook. So much for interest in studies, he thought dolefully. She crawled throughout the house on her stomach. Sometimes, she went about on all fours. If she found a handhold, she would try to stand. She made loud sounds which had no meaning. She made other loud sounds, throwing things and breaking them. And yet, her screams were louder than these sounds.

Every time he entered the house, he found things all over the floor. He shouted at his wife. She rushed about, returning everything to its place. He bought new toys for his daughter all the time, hoping to distract her. No toy kept her entertained for more than a few minutes. She would toss it aside and go searching for something else, ideally something that would break. There was no point shouting at his wife. She put things in order. She carried the baby whenever she could. But she couldn't walk about with the baby at her hip all day. The child didn't want to be carried either. She wanted to crawl as fast as she could. Her mother would have to set her down to do the housework. Kumaresan worried that they wouldn't be able to raise a child like this with discipline. This child was the perfect opposite of his vision of a model child. They would have to keep her at home until she turned two. No school would admit her before that. Perhaps they could put her in hostel. But that was a long time away too. He had told off many, many of his students' parents for not raising their children well. What if he cut a sorry figure before them now? The sight of his daughter barrelling towards him on all fours terrified him. Was this a demon child of some kind?

His wife didn't seem to share his concerns. She kept cooing to the child and making bizarre noises in baby language. Whatever their daughter did, she did not scold or check her. It was she who was spoiling the child, he thought.

On a school holiday, he had removed the mirror from its perch and kept it over a book while searching for something. The child was thrilled. Something she had been trying to get her hands on unsuccessfully for aeons was finally within reach. She rushed to the mirror, took it, and sat down. She brought it towards her mouth with both hands. Kumaresan ran to her in panic. Knowing he would snatch it from her, the child threw the mirror out of his reach. It smashed into a wall. Shards of glass lay scattered over the floor.

This was the last straw. He grabbed the child, ground his teeth and let out a scream. In a moment of madness, he wanted to smash her against the wall just as she had smashed the mirror. His wife rushed to him and grabbed the child. Frightened,

Ridishna began to wail. Her mother drew her close to her chest. Eyes brimming with tears, she turned to Kumaresan and whispered, 'Kozhandhainga' – she's just a baby. It struck him that this was the word she had used most often since her return. Her face and tone disturbed him. He lay on the bed, and fell asleep even as he was thinking about things.

He woke with a start. There was a chill on his face, as if someone were splashing water on it. He opened his eyes. The baby was sitting by him and slapping his face, laughing. It felt like a massage. He closed his eyes and gave himself over to the feeling. Had the baby already forgotten that it was he who had nearly tossed her against the wall? He picked her up gently and put her on his stomach. The child banged both her hands against his chest, over and over again. Her laughter bubbled over with joy.

He looked at the house with the child in the foreground. Everything seemed to be in its rightful place. What did it matter if something taken from this shelf was returned to that one? It was accommodated somewhere or the other. Let everything break. Everything would have to break sometime. He looked about himself with the child's eyes. There was no such thing as order. Refusing to be disciplined was a form of discipline in itself. He laughed along with the child. It struck him then that the gods hadn't given him any task.

6

Baggage

Murugesu and his father were not on talking terms. No one could tell when they had stopped speaking to each other. Now, he was twenty-one and ripe for marriage. His family was looking for a bride. Appa had wanted to marry him off once he turned eighteen. But the law dictated that a groom must be at least twenty-one and a bride at least eighteen in order to be married. Those who flouted this law could be arrested. The family had decided to put off the quest after several people they knew had frightened them with this warning. It would take as little as a text message from an ill-wisher for the authorities to come investigate. One had no shortage of ill-wishers. And so the day Murugesu turned twenty-one, his father began the search in earnest. Yet, through all this, they did not exchange a word.

If they had to convey something to each other, Amma played the conduit.

'Tell your precious son…' Appa would say.

'Go tell your husband…' Murugesu would say.

Or they would speak within each other's earshot without addressing each other directly.

Appa had been nineteen and Amma sixteen when they were married. Appa was an only son, and his mother had wanted to give him ample time to bear fruit for the family tree. Appa did this with gusto. Within five years of marriage, they had three children – a girl and two boys. Raising them was such a strain on the family's resources that Amma and Appa eventually decided they'd multiplied enough.

But breaking all protective barriers, another fetus planted itself in her womb after five years. Amma had irregular periods and didn't keep tabs on her menstrual cycle carefully, so she didn't realize she was pregnant until four months in. She tried taking the abortion pill. The pill only nourished the fetus. They were told it would pose a danger to Amma's life if she had a medical termination five months into the pregnancy, and so they reconciled themselves to four children instead of three. Murugesu was the baby of the family. The youngest of his siblings was six years older than he. His sister and brothers were schoolchildren when he was an infant.

He was just another toy to them. They would come back from school and play with him for a while. Then they would toss him into a corner. If they heard him fussing or crying, each would come over to slap him. The younger of his two brothers would kick him. Amma was the only one who could rescue him from these demons. And so she was his only friend.

As each of his children began to earn a living, Appa got them married off.

'Once someone can make money, it's time to offload that child,' Appa would say. 'We'll be rid of the excess baggage.'

Murugesu found a job right after completing class 12. His eldest brother, who was a mechanic in a lorry workshop, had brought him in as a trainee. His brother could work magic on any engine. Lorries that had to get their FC – fitness certificate – needed a lot of tinkering. Murugesu was an odd-job boy, assisting the mechanics. His brother hoped he would eventually pick up a skill and build a career.

The work on one lorry was nearly over. Only

the lettering remained. The person who would do the lettering with paint was nicknamed 'Writer' in the workshop. The Writer had taken a week off to attend a family function. They tried unsuccessfully to find another Writer. Having overheard the discussion, Murugesu approached his brother hesitantly and asked without making eye contact, 'Shall I do the lettering?'

His brother looked at him in surprise. 'You can write?' 'Really?' 'You?' he asked over and over again.

Murugesu's handwriting was beautiful. It was the content that had been a problem when he was in school. 'Look of a hero, work of a zero,' one of his teachers would often say. Their school was on the outskirts of the village. Before a boundary wall had been built, the school playground had been the village's public toilet. The students' daily chores had included throwing mud over faeces and planting thorns around the playground so outsiders couldn't enter. But the villagers had continued to break in. After years of negotiation, the school had finally won a boundary wall. But this would give their unwelcome visitors something to aim at or something to hide behind. And so the school authorities had decided to commission portraits of gods and politicians and the writing of proverbs and the *Thirukkural* on these walls. The government had refused them funds for the commission, and so the task had fallen to the students.

The first time Murugesu held a brush, he realized the wall provided a more luxurious canvas than his notebooks. When his teacher had seen his handiwork, he had stared and conceded, 'Work of a hero this time, da, Murugesu.'

And yet the artist's own brother had no comprehension of his talent. He could barely believe that Murugesu had good handwriting. But with no other option on offer, Murugesu was given a chance to try his hand.

The lorry was called 'Om Muruga'. He wrote those words first. Lord Muruga did not let him down. Then he wrote in small letters, 'Karikaaliyamman Thunai' – Karikaaliyamman is my strength. He wrote the vehicle's specifications by the side, 'Check me every day' on the radiator, and 'Sound Horn' at the back. Murugesu became the workshop's Writer. He liked his job.

Some lorry drivers wanted portraits of gods painted on their vehicles. He would offer to draw deer or peacocks or motifs for others. He would find various ways to ask vehicles to honk. Some drivers were content with 'SOUND HORN'. He liked writing slogans like 'Sound make, overtake' and 'Honk, pray; Get way'. The job came with some independence – he wasn't paid a fixed amount, but got to negotiate for pay by the letter. He would calculate his fee according to the size of each letter and the length of each slogan. Portraits were liable to an additional charge. Sometimes, he would assess all the work that had to be done on the lorry and give the driver a round sum. He made a decent income. Once he was settled in the job, his father was determined to get him married as soon as possible.

'Once we get rid of this last dog, we won't have to carry baggage. We'll be at peace,' he would say.

Murugesu didn't like any of the prospective brides. It was clear that his father simply wanted to palm him off on some woman. Murugesu had only three criteria – he must like the bride at first sight; his in-laws' home must be conducive to short, peaceful stays; his wife's relatives must be able to rush over to help in case of an emergency. However, his father had no criteria. A girl. That was all. Murugesu had six months to go before he turned twenty-two. He wanted to spend this time perusing brides patiently. His father did not have the patience for this. This was the subject of a snarky exchange every day.

Though neither of them spoke to the other, they did speak at each other. They incited each other till sparks of hatred flew across the room. It was Amma's job to douse the flames.

'His lordship wants his father-in-law to lay down a carpet of flowers for his delicate feet.'

'He should look at his damned face in the mirror.'

Appa had been drinking heavily for seven or eight years. He set aside money from his salary for a 'quarter' every day. It was only the balance that made its way home. 'So his lordship is home? Boys his age find places to hang out. They have friends to roam around with. This damned runt sits inside all day. Holds on to his mother's pallu. Thinks he's a damned suckling,' he would rant as soon as he came home.

It made Murugesu furious. But Amma would intercept him.

'Everyone else complains that their sons never stay home. And here you have a son who goes to work and comes straight home in this day and age, and yet all you do is yell at him,' she would say to her husband. But that didn't mollify Murugesu. 'Drunken dog has to come and bark,' he would snap and go lie down.

This prompted his father to swear and shout ugly insults that the entire street could hear. Although he didn't speak to Murugesu, he could rant about him for hours.

Every time Amma was asked when the two of them had stopped talking, she had a different story to tell.

Murugesu must have been a year and a half old. Amma was alone at home with the child all day. Appa worked at a cement factory. He would eat the leftovers from the previous night and leave early for work. He had to mix cement, sand and gravel to make concrete blocks. Then he and the other labourers had to load the blocks on to trucks to deliver to customers and unload them at the drop-off point. He had been working there for years. Every now and again, he would come home for lunch. Murugesu would watch over Amma carefully. If Appa's hand so much as grazed hers, he would come running and punch his father with his tiny fists.

At first, Appa had found this amusing. He would touch his hand to Amma's cheek just to tease Murugesu. Or he would lean against her back. Or he would hold her hand. Murugesu, whose eyes never strayed from his father, would come running the moment he made contact with Amma. If Appa was standing, the child would hit his legs. If he was sitting, the child would bang Appa on the back. Murugesu's face would turn red and tears of rage would course down his cheeks.

'You think you got here without my laying a hand on your mother, eh?' his father would laugh, pinching his cheeks affectionately.

When the work was light, Appa would come home early for lunch. Once, he came home by eleven in the morning. He lay down on the cot and tried to sleep. But Murugesu was running around him, making a racket. Appa lifted the child on to the bed and tried to lull him to sleep. Murugesu closed his eyes and pretended he was asleep. As soon as his father began to relax, Murugesu sat up and giggled. He did this over and over again until his father decided to divert his attention. Amma was dicing the vegetables, sitting on the floor. Appa went up to her and laid his head on her knee. Murugesu, who was pretending to be asleep, sat up on the cot, ground his teeth, ran to them and slapped his father across the face.

The slap was extraordinarily painful, as if to illustrate the proverb 'Even if the god is small, the puja is grand'. Appa sat up angrily, said, 'Po da!' and pushed him away with a light whack on the cheek. The child stumbled and fell. Picking himself up, he ran back to his father. Appa's lungi had ridden up one leg, leaving his thigh exposed. Murugesu bit him hard. His father jumped up with a yell. A livid bite-shaped mark oozed blood on his thigh. Appa was about to hit the child when Amma pulled Murugesu to her chest to protect him. That was the last time Appa had petted his son, played with him, carried him or spoken to him. He claimed his thigh still bore the scar from the bite.

Sometimes, Amma narrated another incident, from when Murugesu was about six years old. The child was scared of the dark. He wouldn't go to sleep unless a lamp was kept on. If he had to go to the toilet, he wanted Amma to accompany him. He would cuddle up to Amma when he slept.

They lived in a house with a terracotta roof and three small rooms. The largest of these was the living room. They had a little kitchen and a bedroom not much bigger. The two cupboards in the bedroom were not quite spacious enough to store the family's clothes, many of which were scattered about the room. There was one cot with a mattress, which was occupied by Amma and Murugesu. His brothers and sister slept in the living room. Appa's sleeping place wasn't fixed. Usually, he would pull his rope cot on to the road and sleep there. He wasn't the only one. A couple of people from each family slept on the street. During the monsoon and when it was particularly cold, Appa shifted the cot to the living room. Amma would keep the lamp on until Murugesu fell asleep and then switch it off. She couldn't sleep unless it was dark.

Waking up suddenly one night, Murugesu reached for his mother, but the mattress was empty. His mother was missing. The dark seemed to swallow him. He let out a scream of terror and began to sob. 'Amma, Amma,' he wailed, until his mother emerged from the darkness. She switched on the lamp, hugged him and began to comfort him. But everyone in the living room had been startled awake.

'I can't even go to the toilet without you raising a hue and cry,' Amma sighed.

'Goddamn dog, born by an accident and sapping the life out of us!' his father shouted.

Murugesu wanted to go to the toilet. When he stepped out, his father was sitting on the rope cot, smoking a bidi.

'Look at him, walking about after waking everyone up. Cowardly dog…' Appa muttered.

With all the innocence of his age, Murugesu retaliated by imitation – he hocked and spat at his father, and said, '*You're* the dog!'

Wiping the spit from his face, his father declared angrily, 'I'm never going to speak to this insolent dog again.' And they hadn't spoken since.

'How many different stories will you tell me? Which of them is true?' he would ask Amma every time she recounted an incident.

'All of them are true, da,' she would say, and then begin another. 'You must have been about eleven years old…'

'Enough, that's enough. I'm just going to assume I haven't been on talking terms with him ever since I was born,' he would reply.

Amma had five or six instances at hand, and would use each explanation by turn when someone asked why father and son did not speak to each other. The friction between them had reached new levels since the issue of Murugesu's marriage had come up, but Amma was adept at handling the tension. Until that day.

Appa came home tipsy. Murugesu was sitting on the cot in the living room and watching television with great interest. Amma brought groundnuts which she had just boiled. Knowing he was too lazy to shell them, she sat on the floor by him and began to shell them for him. As Amma passed him the boiled groundnuts, he held out his hand for them and tossed them into his mouth, still staring at the television. For some reason, the sight infuriated Appa.

'Ask him to get married quickly and eat out of his wife's hand,' he snapped at Amma.

She didn't take him seriously. Laughing, she said, 'Get him married, then.'

'Am I the one that's turning down every prospective bride for him?' his father said.

'You should find someone he likes,' his mother retorted.

The exchange was quotidian, unworthy of Murugesu's attention.

He'd turned down a bride Appa had found last week. The girl's father had called four or five times to ask whether they could go ahead with the match, and Appa found it difficult to tell him Murugesu had refused.

'What's wrong with the girl we went to see last week? Or her parents, for that matter?' Appa demanded now, as he sat in the portico.

She was the second of three daughters. She had a younger brother too. Murugesu couldn't imagine being one of three sons-in-law. When he thought about a family like that, the film *Middle Class Madhavan* came to mind. Several comic sketches in the film were centred on Vivek's and Vadivelu's visits to their in-laws' home. He couldn't be a Vivek or Vadivelu. And what if a third son-in-law like Charlie turned up? He didn't want anything to do with this family.

He had learnt that the girl's father met Appa every now and again and bought him a 'quarter' at the wine shop. Clearly, he had laid careful plans to fob his daughter off on Murugesu.

This evening, Amma answered on his behalf. 'If he doesn't like her, let him be. Is the village running out of girls? We'll just find another one for him. It's not like he's getting old,' she said gently.

'Aamaam, di. He's not getting old. I am. You've spoiled him rotten.' Suddenly, Appa ground his teeth and dashed into the house. He grabbed Amma by the hair and punched her on the back.

'Aiyo! Aiyo!' Amma cried, trying to free herself from his grasp.

Her struggle further enraged Appa. He did not usually hit his wife in Murugesu's presence. Occasionally, Murugesu would spot bruises on his mother and realize Appa had beaten her. 'See what I do to him!' he would say, starting off in a rage, but Amma would stop him with, 'Po da... even a son has no right to interfere in what goes on between husband and wife.'

Keeping this in mind, Murugesu tried to contain himself now. But as Amma's cries intensified, he stood up and marched over to his father. He pried Appa's hands away from Amma, and said, 'Do you take leave of all your senses when you're drunk?' He twisted Appa's arm, held him in a chokehold and pushed him towards the door. 'Get out!' he said, and gave him a hard shove.

Appa went sprawling on the street, sat up, and

looked about him. All their neighbours seemed to be staring at him. Faces peeped out of every door and window. Appa sat frozen for a few moments and then got up, leaning heavily on his hand.

The entire street heard him say, 'Won't get married because he's kept his mother in a wife's stead, and hits *me* when I ask about it. Motherfucker...'

7

This Will Do

One moment, Kumaresu's mind said, 'Let's go to the wedding.' The next, it demurred. They would be married by now. The ceremony was at a temple, during brahma muhurtam. The festivities were being held at a wedding hall right next to the temple. He had been invited to the celebratory reception and feast, from eight to ten in the morning. Both the bride and groom had gone to school with him, and he had received an invitation from each party. He had already made mental lists of what would happen if he went, and what would happen if he didn't go. Yet, the balance did not tilt to either side.

The wedding venue was a half-hour ride away. His mother had woken him at seven in the morning with a thump on the back. But he did not get up. He lay in bed, awake, his eyes closed. He didn't feel like getting up. After some time, his mother said, 'Says he has to go to a wedding and then sleeps on his stomach, the lazy dog!'

At eight, he rose and got dressed. He began to convince himself it was important to go.

Both of them had been his classmates. Worse, what would she think if he didn't show up? She'd already called him a milksop. If he skipped the wedding, she would likely add 'jellylegs' and 'coward' to the list. They lived in the same town. They couldn't avoid each other forever. Their houses were in the same neighbourhood, and chances were that they would meet every day.

By the time he finished his shower, his mind had gathered strength. His mother had laid out a white shirt and white veshti for the wedding. The veshti's gold border shone bright. He wondered whether he would be overdressed. Then, he decided he had to wear the outfit. His grand appearance would prove that he wasn't upset or disappointed. He wore veshti only when he had to go to functions like this, and so he was out of practice. It took him a long time to tie it to his satisfaction.

It was half past nine before he was ready to leave.

'They invite him for breakfast, and he lands up for lunch. They're going to scrape the bowl and throw the remains at the dog that showed up at the end of the feast,' his mother muttered loud enough for him to hear.

'Is a wedding all about the food?' he shot back, getting on his motorcycle. It was an Enfield Bullet. It had only been six months since he'd bought it. He had often imagined her riding pillion, her arm around his waist. He had lost out. Well, it was her loss, really. He didn't want to leave her a souvenir of himself by giving them a wedding gift and decided to give them money in an envelope instead. She would have no use for memories of him.

She had been his classmate for ten years. The school was within walking distance of home. He had known her since she had bumbled her way to class, wiping her dripping nose with her skirt. It was in class 5 that he had begun to feel a strange fondness for her. Every night, he would hide some of the gravy from dinner to share with her at lunch the next day. She also got a share of the crunchy snacks his father bought.

At the time, his nickname in school was 'thinni pandaaram' – food junkie. He hated the name. If someone called him that, he would give chase until he had cornered the offender. She usually addressed him as 'Dei, thinni!' But he never objected. He liked hearing her call him that way. Back then, her baby fat was all stored in her stomach, and so he would retort with, 'Ennadi, panni?' – What is it, pig? She never took offence either.

She attained maturity in class 7. There was a small function at her home, which he attended. When he saw her, all dressed up and sitting on the chair, it struck him that she no longer looked like a child. Was she really this beautiful? He assumed her family would stop sending her to school, as most girls' families did. But she didn't drop out. She continued to call him 'Dei, thinni!' But he wasn't able to bring himself to call her 'panni'. Her waist had shrunk. Her face glowed. But she was cheekier than ever. He felt an uncontrollable urge to throw his arms around her and hold her tight. He would do that before the year was out, he decided. That didn't happen. His mind hesitated to obey the commands of his body.

They moved to a different school for classes 9 and 10. The groom joined them in class 9. He had blended into the background when they were in school, and Kumaresu thought of him as 'the wallflower'. The wallflower would come to school, sit, and leave for the day. Kumaresu barely registered his presence. He was busy suffering in silence, longing to tell her of his love and failing to find the courage. His friend Dheeresh, who was his sole confidante at the time, tried nudging him into the confession. He could talk to her about anything, but he couldn't declare his love for her. Perhaps it was because he knew he couldn't take a rejection. Their schooldays ended without his telling her how he felt.

He passed the class 10 maths paper with a high score. He was a whiz at maths. He solved science problems which involved mathematical calculations admirably, but drew a blank elsewhere. Similarly, he excelled in Tamil grammar. His teachers were bewildered by his selective virtuosity. He wasn't interested in any other subject. He didn't pass any of the other papers. His mother hoped she could send him to work if he managed to graduate class 10. He sat home for six months and studied for a second attempt. Then he went to a private coaching centre for six months. He passed Tamil and social science this time. He couldn't bring himself to study for the other exams.

'Lazy dog sleeps when I ask him to study,' his mother lamented.

He said he would study while working, and joined an egg company. He had to load crates of eggs on to lorries. His work would begin in the afternoon and stretch into the night. The muscles on his arms got into knots from the effort of lifting the crates. He had blisters on his feet from walking. His older colleagues would snap, 'Young blood, and such a slob!' The lorries left for the stores three days a week. He only had to work on those days.

Once, the proprietor of the company came to the loading point. When he asked how many crates had been loaded and how many remained, Kumaresu was able to answer accurately. The proprietor asked him for a couple of other details, and he answered. It seemed to him that the proprietor was testing him. The proprietor then asked about Kumaresu's educational qualifications. Kumaresu answered truthfully.

'Come and see me in the office tomorrow,' the proprietor said and left.

His colleagues told him he was likely to be offered the position of travelling accountant. An accountant had to accompany the lorry on its journey. Each lorry distributed the eggs to stores in three or four towns. The accountant's task was to keep count of how many eggs each shop stocked, and ensure payment for the eggs that had been sold earlier. He had to be firm with those who owed money. Then he had to return to the office and deposit the money safely. One needed to be shrewd, sound with calculations and honest to be recruited for the job. Kumaresu wasn't sure he should accept. He was the only son of the family, with two older sisters. And so his mother decreed, 'The guard dog can stay home, there's no need to wander the streets.'

He went to meet the proprietor the next day. The office was a single room, tucked into a little street in that little town. The proprietor asked him to sit in a chair across from him and passed him some notebooks. He gave him details of records that had to be maintained and told him how to tally the accounts. Kumaresu was quick on the uptake. He rarely needed the calculator. He finished his tally and looked up to see that tea had arrived and was getting cold on the table. The proprietor examined his work for a long time. He couldn't spot a single error. Kumaresu's handwriting was impeccable too.

The proprietor asked him to come to office the next day, and the next. The travelling accountants brought the money to the office, and submitted their calculations. The proprietor asked him to receive, count and check the money against the calculations, and stayed on to observe. This went on for two weeks. Then, the proprietor told him he would be taking over as manager – a role the proprietor himself had assumed all this while – and had a table and chair assigned to Kumaresu. It appeared the proprietor had been intending to retire for some time and had been looking for someone to take over so he could sit back and enjoy the lifestyle he had earned. His children were all settled abroad. And so Kumaresu became manager of a company at seventeen.

She, too, discontinued her studies after class 10. She went to work at a shop whose owner was a friend of her father's. The shop sold timepieces. It also had a division that was responsible for maintenance and repair. She began with changing the cells, and went on to learn several aspects of watch and clock repair. Kumaresu visited the shop every now and again. He only ever gifted clocks and watches to people. If any of his friends wanted to buy or repair a watch, he would take them to the shop. If he felt like seeing her face, he would buy a watch or clock. Clocks stared from every part of every wall of his home. His mother had sent a few to the homes of his sisters too. Every time she asked, 'Why do we need so many clocks?' he would reply, 'Time is the most important thing in the world. One needs to be able to tell the time at a glance.' 'Yes, of course. The dog doesn't have the time to stand in one place, doesn't have any work to do either, and has to know the time. Most of the clocks don't have cells. *Time is the most important thing in the world*, it seems,' his mother would mutter.

Over the years he visited the shop, she noticed the little changes in him. He had progressed from a gearless scooter to an Enfield Bullet. A longish gold chain had made its way around his neck. A watch shone on one wrist and a bracelet on the other. He had begun to wear branded clothing. The girl who could see his growing prosperity was blind to his love. She had simply thought he was coming to visit and chat with a long-time friend.

It was only about a year ago that she'd realized how he felt about her.

He chanced upon her walking down the road one day and asked her to get on his bike. She had never ridden a Bullet before, and was tempted. She climbed up behind him. As soon as she mounted the bike, he was overcome with shyness. Everyone seemed to be staring at them. He lowered his eyes and rode through the streets. Slowly, the pride of riding a motorcycle that induced everyone's envy with a pillion rider who induced everyone's envy lifted his gaze, and he began to feel smug. He wasn't sure how fast she'd like to go, and so he rode relatively slowly. He insisted on stopping at a restaurant, and took her to the air-conditioned section.

She had never been to such a place. He asked her what she'd like to eat, and placed the order.

'So you're still a thinni pandaaram, is it, da?' she laughed, and then asked easily, 'So, tell me – you're a rich guy now. When are you getting married?'

The circumstances gave him the courage he had never before found. 'If you say yes, we can get married right away,' he replied.

She looked at him, puzzled.

He put it to her directly. 'Do you really not understand? I'm always hovering about you. I've been at it for years. Can you not see why?'

For the first time, she gave it some thought. All this while, it had seemed perfectly normal for a boy she'd been to school with for ten years to drop in for a chat every now and again. She had never seen him as anything but the Kumaresu from school. He was her old friend from kindergarten, and she still liked talking to that little boy.

'It's because of you that I've bought a hundred and twenty-four timepieces so far.' He told her the story of how he had fallen in love with her in class 5 and had never fallen out of love since. Somehow, he found the words that day, with no hesitation and no fear.

She ate as she listened. Then she briefed him on her situation. She didn't have much faith in love. Her family circumstances could have contributed to this. Her parents had had several daughters in their quest to produce a son. She was the third of five girls. There had been two or three cases of female infanticide and four or five of feticide. It was only after the doctor had warned that her mother would die if she carried another baby that her father had given up. If she had a love marriage, it would be hard for her parents to get her younger sisters married. It could also cause trouble for her older sisters with their in-laws. There was another problem – he and she were of different castes. He was a rung below in the caste hierarchy. Her parents would not agree to this. She had no wish to elope and pay the price for defying her family all her life. She saw his despondent face and consoled him with, 'You'll find a more suitable girl than me.'

But he looked as if all the life had faded out of him. She took pity on him and added a suggestion. Just as he had found the courage to speak up today, he must find the courage to come home with his parents and ask for her hand in marriage. If her parents gave their consent, she was willing to marry him.

'Come if you can,' she said, as if throwing him a challenge. 'But I know you're a milksop.'

Her family was looking for a groom for her. She had no great expectations. If her family liked someone, she would agree to marry that person.

As she took her leave of him, she said, 'Don't worry. All this won't matter after marriage.'

He couldn't figure out what she'd meant. He

mulled it over and tried interpreting it in various ways. It only confused him.

How could a girl of her age feel no excitement at the thought of love? Surely, she must have been flattered that a boy had been in love with her since class 5? How could she be so unmoved? She had philosophized as if she had seen all there was to see in the world and lived out her life, and then walked away as if it were no big deal. Had she not seen the desire in his eyes as he spoke to her in the shop day after day, year after year? Even the most casual conversation would surely betray the tenderness of a lover for the girl of his dreams? Or had he failed to convey this love and desire and tenderness when he had looked at her? Had he behaved like a regular customer every time he had visited the shop? When they passed each other on the street, had he worn the nonchalance of a stranger?

He found solace in one detail – she had not rejected him outright. She was willing to marry him. Thankfully, she hadn't belted out a filmy dialogue along the lines of 'You're like a brother to me'. He wondered whether he could explain his predicament to his parents and ask them to approach her family with a formal proposal. Would they agree to this? 'The stray dog wants a golden leash, is it?' his mother would snarl. That was how his mother showed her affection for the son who had been an answer to their prayers – she referred to him as a dog at least once a day.

Her speech had stirred thoughts that had never crossed his mind in all these years. It struck him that she was even more skilled at calculation than he was. She had a point – it made little sense to provoke a caste which had taken upon itself the holy duty of murdering lovers. Perhaps she had hidden her love for him in order to spare him. There was no way he could make a formal proposal to her parents. She wouldn't break ties with them either. What could he do? He conjured various scenarios as he weighed his options. This only discombobulated him. Must he let go of this love?

He slept poorly for days on end. He stopped going to the clock shop. The hundred and twenty-fifth timepiece was never bought. If he happened to pass by the shop, he would peek inside from afar. It was as if a spotlight shone on her wherever she stood. His arms would long to turn into those rays of light and caress her. He would be rooted to the spot, miserable.

He told his friend Dheeresh about their conversation at the restaurant.

'I thought the puppy love would only spill out when you were a pensioner. Not bad, you did tell her!' he teased. Dheeresh's bright idea was to kidnap her, cart her to a temple and tie a thaali around her neck. Forcing her into marriage didn't seem right to Kumaresu. They would have to return to the same town after the deed was done. How would they deal with the aftermath?

Before he could recover from his stupor, she landed up with her wedding invitation. The groom was the wallflower from classes 9 and 10. His eyes hurt when he envisioned them standing together.

'You're going to marry that wallflower?' he couldn't stop himself from asking.

'If I were about to marry you, someone would have asked me if I'm going to marry that thinni,' she laughed. 'Come to the wedding. And don't buy me a clock, get me something else. Money would be ideal.'

The wallflower came home with an invitation too. It was clear that there was nothing he could do anymore. The only dilemma which presented itself now was: should he go to the wedding or stay away?

Having made his decision and arrived at the wedding hall, he found the feast was nearly over. The bride and groom were about to get off the stage.

Dheeresh, who was leaving the venue, ran into him outside.

'Look at you, dressed like the groom and arriving later than the groom,' he laughed, slapping him on the back. Dheeresh accompanied him to the stage. He handed over the envelope to her.

'No more clocks,' he said.

It wasn't clear whether she had heard him. 'Go eat,' she said.

The dining hall was nearly empty. Banana leaves had been laid out on only one of the rows of tables. The latecomers were settling down in this row. He joined them. Just as he was sprinkling water on the leaf before the meal, the bride and groom arrived.

'What kind of thinni pandaaram eats after everyone else?' she laughed, and sat next to him.

The fragrance of flowers from her hair took his

breath away. The groom, who was seated on her other side, had disappeared from his view. It was just the two of them now.

They laughed together. She called for his plate to be filled every time he had nearly finished. He had no clue what he had eaten. She got up first. He followed her. If Dheeresh hadn't tugged at his arm, he wouldn't have come out of his reverie.

'Go wash your hands,' Dheeresh said, pointing to the tap.

When he returned from washing his hands, Dheeresh said, 'I've sent you photos. Look.'

He reached for his phone with his wet hands and looked. The pictures had been taken when they were eating. There were five or six photos of Kumaresu with her. There was no one else in the frame. He looked like the groom. She was the bride. One of the photos had captured an incredible moment – the two of them were laughing together, with all the bliss of newly-weds.

'This will do. This will do for me, da,' he said and pulled his friend into a grateful hug.

8

Ice Apple

Murugesu was grazing the sheep. Together with the lambs, they made a flock of around thirty. His father had been taking them to graze until a year ago. For as long as Murugesu had been in school, the boy had taken the sheep out at dawn for a couple of hours and left for his school after seeing them back into their pens. In the evenings, he had gone straight from school to their grazing area and relieved his father from duty. After graduating from school, he had enrolled in a college and dropped out within six months.

'What is this, you've left a boy of this generation to graze sheep,' someone would comment every now and again.

Appa would answer cheerfully, 'It's our hereditary profession, isn't it? It appears to be our destiny.' He would add, 'He finished his twelfth. I wanted him to study further, and sent him off to college. The donkey told me that every time he saw the students walk about in flocks, he was reminded of our sheep, and it's all the same to him. He came back here.'

It was Appa who had taught his son the nuances of sheep farming and grazing. Once he had handed over his responsibilities to Murugesu, he'd begun to look for other work. He helped his neighbours out with agricultural tasks like seeding and harvesting. For one week of each month, he would join the government's 100-day labour scheme.

'Ada...all we do is pluck a few blades of grass here and there, and then sit down in the shade to talk,' Appa said. 'Whatever we do, we're entitled to payment. Looks like government service is written in my stars.'

He also visited two markets each week to trade sheep. The butchers would sniff out rams and make their ways home to fetch them. Appa took pregnant sheep and baby lambs to the market to sell. He preferred his new routine to what he called 'lying at the feet of sheep'.

'For years, the sheep have been my entire world. Now, my son has taken over and sent me out into the real world,' Appa often said proudly.

Every now and again, he would go meet Murugesu at the grazing area and gossip with his son for a while. Appa was a good climber. Murugesu couldn't climb trees. This was a sore point with Appa. If only Murugesu could climb, he would be able to scale the gulmohur, portia and commiphora trees and cut down leaves for the sheep. He couldn't do this, and so he shook the branches of the karuvelam trees as high as he could reach. When Appa visited, he would climb trees and cut down branches for the sheep. As he climbed, he would mutter to himself, 'A tiger's found its way into a family of cats just to embarrass us.' He made sure Murugesu did not hear this. The boy could answer back.

Murugesu had climbed various kinds of trees in his childhood. He could balance himself on neem branches, loop ropes over the thinnest stalks at the top of the tree, shake the ropes and call, 'There's a ghost in the tree!'

It was Appa who had ruined everything. He'd decided to teach Murugesu to climb the palm tree when he was about ten years old. The boy loved ice apples, and if he learnt to climb the palm, he could pick them himself.

Appa taught him two ways to climb. You had to fasten a rope around your feet. If you splayed your legs while climbing, you would lose your grip. Appa used a rope woven into an oval shape, around which palm fibres had been wound. He joined the ends to make a grip for his feet and climbed the palm tree. He pressed his chest against the trunk as he climbed. This technique would make the chest sore from friction with the bark. It was hard to protect your chest while climbing this way. The palm, ever impartial, wounded everyone who scaled it.

The better technique was to use your hands rather than your chest as the grip. This also allowed you to climb faster. Appa was a natural. Once he had reached the top, he would fool around. He would negotiate past the serrated edges of the leaves and seat himself on the spathes, within reach of bunches of ice apples. He would cut into one ice apple from each bunch and sample its juice. He told Murugesu this was how one checked for quality. The boy, who was waiting to suck on the ice apples, would feel irritated as he stood at the bottom of the tree, watching his father sample fruit after fruit.

It was only after he had lost all patience and said, 'I'm leaving, Appa,' that his father would get around to cutting down the bunches for him.

Appa taught him only the first method of climbing in the beginning – gripping the trunk with one's chest. Halfway up the tree, Murugesu's hands began to tremble. By the time he got back down, his legs were shaking too.

'Jellylegs!' Appa laughed.

Murugesu began to climb when his father was not around, and eventually succeeded in reaching the top of the tree. Thrilled with his feat, he showed off to his father one day. Appa was delighted. He asked Murugesu to climb with the sickle fastened to his back, and taught him how to balance himself on the spathes and cut down ice apple bunches from his perch.

Murugesu proved to be a keen learner. One day, his father told him to avoid climbing the palm when the ice apples were ripening. Snakes were drawn by the smell of fruit, and often lay coiled on the spathes. If one spotted a snake, one must either possess the instinct to cut it in half with the sickle or the speed to clamber down before the snake could bite. Appa took only half the time to get down as he did to climb up. He showed Murugesu how to come down even faster. It was as if Appa's hands were sliding down a smooth trunk – he glided to the ground effortlessly. Murugesu found this fascinating.

One day, as Murugesu was climbing down in his leisurely way, after having cut down the ice apple bunches, his father suddenly shouted, 'Dei! Snake! Snake!'

In his panic, Murugesu forgot how to slide down the trunk. He let go and fell to the ground, from more than halfway up the tree, screaming, 'Aiyo!' He hit the mud, which had just been dug up for seeding. The earth received him as if on a bed of flowers. But the shock of falling had made him catch his breath. There was nobody around to help. His father rushed to him, carried him to the shade, and set him down. Then Appa broke open an ice apple and splashed the juice on the boy's face and wet his tongue with the pulp.

Murugesu tried to raise himself up slowly. He began to cry. He couldn't move. Appa stood him up and asked him to shake out his arms and legs. It was slow and painful, but he was able to do it.

'My kanna, nothing has happened to you, da.

Bhoomadevi held you in her grasp and saved you. There's a force looking after you. Don't worry, kanna,' Appa said. He pulled the boy's head to his lap, and found himself wanting to cry like his son. He rambled on incoherently as he picked the juiciest ice apples for Murugesu. He made his son eat them, and spread the juice all over the boy's body to soothe his bruises.

Appa told Amma that Murugesu had let go of his grip on the trunk about six feet from the ground and fallen. Murugesu was still in tears, but he did not say a word to his mother. He lay in bed for ten days. There were bruises all over his body. His mother gave him warm baths and fashioned hot compresses from cloth for him. Under her care, he recovered. Appa showered him with love. His gratitude to the boy for not telling on him filled him with guilt and compassion. He bought him eggs and meat. He trapped baby pigeons, made soup from the tender flesh and fed it to his son. Murugesu came back to his usual self. But he never climbed a tree again.

The idea of climbing made him shake. Even going near a tree put a tremor in his legs. He didn't dare climb even the neem tree. He couldn't bring himself to look up at the palmyras. He had no recollection of what had passed between his letting go of the trunk and hitting the ground. If only he could recall those moments, he might be able to resolve the triggers and overcome his fear. He might be able to climb trees again. But chasing the memory felt like trying to catch a dream that disappears even as one strains to hold on to its remnants. Eventually, he decided not to convince himself to climb trees again. Appa tried everything.

'Look, I'm lighting a bidi…let's say I get burnt from the match. Can I stop lighting bidis for the rest of my life? I'll just be careful the next time I strike a match. That's all, isn't it?' he said once.

'Lighting a bidi is the same thing as climbing a tree, is it?' Murugesu snapped.

'You don't ever have to climb a tree, kanna. Don't people who can't climb trees survive in this world?' Amma said.

This line became a favourite of Murugesu's, and he used it to counter Appa's arguments. Appa would mumble and mutter words he couldn't make out. If he asked, Appa would say, 'Nothing, po da.'

It hurt Appa that his son couldn't climb trees. When Murugesu said he would quit college and take over the grazing, Appa's first thought was, 'But he can't climb trees.' Sometimes, the anxiety would propel his legs to the grazing area where Murugesu sat, and he would climb the trees himself to cut down leaves for the flock. His mouth would form words of reproach, sometimes fondly and sometimes with irritation. Murugesu would pretend not to hear. He was glad Appa hadn't objected when he'd asked to quit college and take over the flock; he wasn't going to rock the boat by getting drawn into a quarrel.

Murugesu liked his job. Watching sheep seemed better use of one's time than interacting with people. He got into a routine. He would wake up at the crack of dawn, splash water on his face to wash the sleep from his eyes, take a milking vessel from the house and head to the pen. If there was only one lamb at the time, he would carry the little one in his arms, holding it against his chest for warmth. If there was more than one lamb, he would tuck them into a basket and carry it on his head to the pen. Once he reached the pen, he would set the farm dog loose. The dog would run around in delight. The ewes and lambs would set up a great bleating at the sight of each other. Once he set the lambs down, they would run to their mothers and bump their heads with joy as they settled in to feed. He would milk an ewe whose lambs had been weaned. They were used to him, and didn't fuss. He would take the milk back to the house for coffee. Sheep's milk was ideal for coffee.

Every now and again, his mother would shake her head and say, 'How do you drink coffee with this milk?'

'Drink it and see,' he laughed once.

'You should have been born a lamb,' Amma laughed back.

He would choose a large tumbler and spend half an hour under the neem tree, sipping his coffee. Then, armed with a bottle of water, a book and a length of cloth, he would set off with the flock to the grazing area before the sun's light turned to heat. The sheep were hungry and would scamper away to eat if he didn't drive them quickly. Once they had reached the grazing spot, he would lie down in the shade of a tree and open his book. He liked reading. Once a month, he took the afternoon off. On full moon days, Appa was in charge of the evening graze, and Murugesu was free. The boy boarded the bus to the nearest town, where he spent some time browsing the government library and various bookstores. He would choose the books he wanted, go to the cinema to watch a film, eat some parotta at a favourite joint, and then return home. He got off on the highway and walked the rest of the way. The moonlight enveloped him like an umbrella, and he wished the walk would never end. This was his one outing.

Even as he read, he would keep an ear tuned to the bleating of the sheep. As the flock moved to fresh grazing points, he changed trees to stay near them. He would chew on fruits he plucked and watch the birds. If he felt sleepy, he would grant himself a power nap. As the sun rose, the sheep began to get thirsty. He would count them as he herded the flock together, and drive them back home once he'd gathered them all.

The other herders would just be making their way to the grazing point as he was returning. He encountered at least a couple on his way back, and they had to go to pains to separate their flock. His flock was the largest in the area. The other farmers had ten, perhaps fifteen, animals each. The herders were all much older than he.

'You're already done by the time we finish our work at the farm and come out with the sheep,' they would say yearningly, when they met him.

'My sheep always get the first crop,' he would laugh. 'Yours only get their leftovers!'

'Look how he talks! This is what an education will give you,' they would laugh back, poking his cheeks.

Murugesu filled the water troughs in the pen to entice the flock inside. They would spread out after drinking their fill and nod off. It was only then that he had time to himself. He would eat breakfast, do odd jobs around the house, lie down and read until he fell asleep himself. He woke at three in the afternoon, had lunch, and let the sheep out once the sun's heat had abated a little.

The evening graze was by the lake. The other herders were there too. He sat down with them for a chat. The old men had interesting stories to tell. When the sun was but a line on the horizon, he would gather his flock again. The sheep liked to snack on the grass on their way back. They were quiet, walking lazily towards the farm. He walked slowly too, just keeping up with them. They loitered about until nightfall. Even when they couldn't see the grass, they could sniff it out. It was the little lambs that herded the flock back to the farm, anxious for their mothers to suckle them.

Murugesu's work didn't end with putting the sheep back in the pen. The more adventurous of the sheep had their forelegs tied together with the rope looped over their necks, so they couldn't run too far. He had to untie them. The lone ram in the flock was a bully – he would chase the ewes and lambs if he were left to his own devices. And so Murugesu had to tie him to a pole. They had made one from iron, because the ram was strong enough to pull a wooden pole loose. The rope was of a length that gave him some space to move about, while sparing his penmates any distress.

Murugesu carried the baby lambs to the farmstead. He could hear the bleating of their mothers right until he reached the door. The farm dog was always waiting, wagging his tail furiously, having sensed Murugesu's arrival. Amma had kept the dog's meal ready. Murugesu would carry the food out and walk with the dog to the pen. The dog would run ahead, looking back every now and again. Once he'd reached his bowl, he would stop and look expectantly at Murugesu, his entire lower body wagging with his tail. The moment Murugesu emptied the food into the bowl, the dog would dive in. Amma usually threw in some fish with the rice, and so the dog licked his bowl clean. Murugesu would chain the dog for the night, walk around the pen to make sure everything was all right and then return home. Dinner, television, sleep. A good night's sleep.

His mother had a constant complaint – who would want their daughter to marry a boy who raised sheep for a living? He made more money than people who worked in offices even if he sold two lambs a month. But who took this into account?

Murugesu said, 'Let it go, Amma. Our leader has promised to make sheep rearing a government job. Soon, I'll be a government employee. A thousand people will fight each other to get their daughters married to me.'

But they couldn't postpone their search for a bride until that day dawned. Appa took the bride hunt up as a job, running concurrent with his 100-day government service. One had to tell a few people so word would get around.

'The boy doesn't have a single bad habit. He's

always got his nose in a book. He didn't like the idea of working for anyone else. He wanted to be his own boss. He says he doesn't have to answer to anyone. He won't let us sell a single lamb. He says he's going to grow the flock, so that we have a hundred sheep within five–six years. My holdings of an acre and a half won't be enough to feed such a large flock!' Appa would boast. Finally, he would add, 'We don't want dowry. All we want is a girl. Find out and let us know?'

One day, as Appa was giving his colleagues this spiel, one of them sighed. 'Oh, don't start off again. Boys who wear jeans and go to work in town have a hard time finding a bride. You think your son who wanders about in lungi and vest is going to find a girl? The girls will call him insane. Because you asked, I went and spoke on your behalf to a girl's parents. Even as we were speaking, the girl came right out and asked me how anyone could sleep next to a man who's spent the whole day with sheep. Ask your son to go find some other work.'

Appa couldn't believe his ears. How had the man spoken so plainly to his face? Would Murugesu find a girl at all? Where could they search for a bride? Should they say the boy was a farmer rather than go into the specifics? Perhaps that sounded more respectable? These thoughts tore through his mind as he walked to the TASMAC shop. He downed a 'cutting' and went to the grazing area, sickle in hand.

'The ice apples are begging to be cut down from this palm. Doesn't know how to climb. Could at least have asked me to climb the tree and cut them, no? What a boy! Damned dog in the manger!' He hocked and spat as he began to climb.

Murugesu didn't say a word.

'You don't eat them if you don't want to. But shouldn't you know the sheep would die for a taste?' Appa called.

His voice boomed from the top of the tree, loud enough for the entire village to hear.

Sheep would get through the ice apples, casing and all, in seconds. Appa cut down two bunches alone and began his descent. Murugesu did not budge. The sheep began to run towards the bunches.

'Herd the sheep together. Standing like a damned dunce!' Appa cried.

Murugesu drove the sheep away.

Appa began to shave away the casings from the ice apples on one of the bunches. The sheep ached to get a taste. Murugesu stood guard, keeping them in a herd.

'Here, suck on these. Don't know how to climb, but know how to eat, don't you?' his father said snidely, pushing a couple of ice apples towards him.

Murugesu didn't want to so much as touch the ice apples.

'Come eat, da. Aiyya has taken umbrage, is it? Slight on your dignity, eh? Would anyone with dignity choose to graze sheep?' Appa went on.

Murugesu had had enough. He moved away as if chasing a lamb that had broken rank. Without their herder to discipline them, the sheep ran towards Appa. Some began to chew the ice apples on the ground. Others went for the bunch he was holding. One bit the ice apple in his other hand. Appa was surrounded by the sheep. Trying in vain to escape the mob closing in on him, he cried, 'Thuy! Thuy!' But the sheep kept coming. He sank into their depths, his head disappearing from view. Only his 'Thuy! Thuy!' was heard.

Appa was brought to his knees, and then pressed to the floor. Sheep were all over his body.

Murugesu, who had been watching in silence all this while, came to his senses and raised his staff. 'Chhi! Brainless sheep!' he cried, as he swung the stick over the heads of his flock.

9

Pondaatti

Murugesu woke only at eight. His hands felt for his phone right away. She had texted him at six in the morning, saying she would be home alone that day and asking him to come over for lunch. He was excited. 'Really? Shall I come over?' he texted back. He couldn't take his eyes off the phone for the next few minutes. There was no reply. She must be busy. She lived with her parents, older sister and younger brother. They were probably getting ready to leave. She would see them off and then reply, or perhaps call.

He went outside, his phone in hand. He stared at it as he brushed his teeth. He took it with him into the toilet too. The phone would beep when he got a text. He knew this, but he was not satisfied unless he kept checking. So far, they had only met in public places. She had called him home today. It couldn't be just for food. He had tried several times, and she had refused. He'd promised her there would be no problems, they would see that they didn't get into trouble before marriage. She wouldn't budge. She insisted they had to wait until marriage. All he had permission to do was walk by her side, slip an arm around her waist, and kiss her on the cheek. This wasn't enough.

It had been over six months since they had begun to hang out, and yet she didn't entirely trust him.

'If something *does* happen, we can get married right away,' he had said. He'd also said, 'If we can do this only after marriage, let's get married now.' He was happy to talk to both sets of parents and ask permission. He was happy to elope too. He had told some of his friends to be ready to help should the circumstance arise. He was the middle child in his family. His older sister was married. His younger brother was in school. Only the two sons remained with their parents at home. He would have no trouble convincing his parents to get him married.

He was twenty-two years old. Appa had been saying they would be done with one responsibility if they married him off. He had been non-committal thus far. He was committed to her. The problem was her sister. For as long as the older daughter was unmarried, the family would not get the younger one married. If she eloped, her sister would have trouble finding a groom because of the social stigma. Her sister would be married within the year, and then there would be no problem, she had said. Surely he could hold on for a year?

He often heaved a dramatic sigh of longing when he looked at her or was speaking to her. She would laugh. 'If you're in such a hurry, marry Akka,' she'd said once. 'Am I the one who's unwilling?' he'd retorted. 'Ask her if she'll marry me.'

It was her akka he had first met. That story dated back to a year and a half earlier. He had begun working in the construction business, handling thermomechanically treated bars. He would take a bus from his home on the outskirts of town to meet his boss. He reported to a foreman who worked under the construction engineer. They would send him to different sites for work. Sometimes, it was walking distance. At other times, he would have to take another bus to get to the site. He had to be at the construction site by ten in the morning. Two or three others worked with him. They had to cut, bend and bind the

TMT bars. The more experienced workers would see to the measurement and placement of the bars. He was paid 600 rupees a day. He had a weekly off on Sundays. He could take other days off if he wanted to. If he showed up for work, he was paid.

He usually took the nine-thirty bus. Her akka used to take the same bus. He'd figured out that her home was at the stop after his. He'd been attracted to her the moment he had set eyes on her. But she wore a sullen expression on her face all the time. He wondered if she ever smiled. He would sigh to his friends, 'Couldn't god have spared a smile for a face so beautiful?' He had tried chatting her up a couple of times. She didn't give him the time of day. She worked at a Xerox shop. He had visited a few times. Once, when he had approached her, she'd snapped, 'Shut up and get lost. Don't try these tricks with me!' and walked away quickly.

When he'd told a colleague about the exchange and remarked, 'Do girls really talk like this?' his friend had laughed, 'Are you sure your fly wasn't open?'

Murugesu hadn't so much as glanced at her after the incident. She had changed her shift at the shop too. If they happened to run into each other, his hand would unconsciously check his zip.

About eight months after this, he had met her younger sister entirely by chance, without knowing they were related. She was working at a 'fancy store' because she had failed her English exam in class 10 and couldn't study further.

Not long after they had started seeing each other, her sister had spotted them together near the fancy store. When she'd returned home, her sister had greeted her with, 'I've slippered that guy and chased him away. Why are you hanging out with him?'

'He's not that sort of guy,' she had replied.

'Yeah, right, you just watch – he's going to knock you up and ditch you. Then you'll know what a cheat he is!' her sister had said furiously, and then kept her peace.

Every time he tried to take things a little further, her sister's words would pop into her mind. 'Will you cheat me like Akka said?' 'Will you knock me up and ditch me like Akka said?' she would ask.

This irritated him. This akka of hers said things he had never imagined women could say.

Sometimes, she would tease him, saying, 'You're

the guy whom my sister slippered and chased away, aren't you?'

'Come, let's go ask her. If it's true that she's slippered me, I'll hang myself to death right away,' he would snap. Her sister was out to humiliate him, and made up all sorts of nonsense, he thought. 'She's jealous that I like you. She's regretting the fact that she let a stud like me slip. That's why she's saying all this shit about me,' he said.

Just speaking of her sister created tensions between the two of them.

The boys of that area had nicknamed her sister 'Musudu' – sourpuss. 'Don't speak about that musudu. Just tell me when her marriage is fixed, that's all I care about,' he would say.

She told him her sister had begun to learn the basics of computer science at the DTP centre where she worked, and had insisted that there would be no talk of marriage until she had upskilled herself.

'When is Musudu going to learn her work, when do we go about our work?' he would say, making a pitiable face.

'You only ever think of one thing!' she would laugh, and box him playfully.

It was evident that she was tempted too. But she was scared. 'Don't be afraid,' he'd said often enough. 'I'll buy a manjakayaru and tie it around your neck at the Muruga temple, don't worry.' But she remained apprehensive.

How had her fears dissipated today? She had actually invited him home. He marvelled at this, even as he got ready for the day. He went out to buy an expensive brand of soap. He lathered himself thrice with it when he showered. The fragrance was enticing even to him. He imagined showering with her. He tried on all the shirts and trousers he owned, in various combinations. None was entirely satisfactory, but he finally settled on a set of clothes. If only he had known a day earlier, he could have bought a new shirt and trousers. He chose undergarments that had no holes and looked fairly new. He combed, tousled and re-combed his hair several times. He sprayed on cologne with a subtle scent of sandalwood.

Once he was dressed, he didn't know what to do. He kept checking his phone. He sent her another text, saying simply '???????????' Would she call him or not? Had she been kidding? Was she playing him? He wasn't able to eat. It was Sunday, and he could smell a roast cooking in the kitchen. He couldn't stop looking at his phone. He picked at the meatballs his mother gave him with rice. 'Always walking about like he's possessed,' he vaguely heard his mother say.

At eleven-thirty, she called him. She asked him to come home after an hour, and to make sure no one saw him enter.

Her house was at the intersection of two streets. Their landlord lived in the street that ran south of the house. There were five row houses on the street that ran east. These houses had a kitchen, bedroom and a little hall each, with shared bathrooms and toilets. Hers was the second house on the row. Not many people would be about in the afternoon. But she warned him to look around carefully before coming inside.

'There's no one at home, and I want to cook for you myself. Don't read too much into this, that's all you're getting,' she giggled on the phone. The giggle seemed to hold promise.

He left right away. He didn't have a two-wheeler. He had been saving to buy one. But Appa had said the bride's family would buy him one when he married. Murugesu had told Appa he had to get with the times – no one would offer a bride to a man who didn't already have a two-wheeler. He had considered buying a motorcycle on EMI. It was she who had convinced him to postpone the purchase, asking him to save for their wedding instead. He could borrow a motorcycle from one of his friends. But he couldn't ride it up to her front door. Where could he park it without attracting attention?

He decided to take the bus. He was bathed in sweat by the time he rode the one stop to hers. He wiped furiously with his handkerchief, but he kept perspiring. Was it from the heat or his nervousness, he wondered. He sat under the shade at the bus shelter for a bit. All he needed to do was enter her house, all he needed to do was see her. He could relax after that.

The streets were empty. A lone buffalo had been tied with a long rope to a post so it could graze. It looked at him and bellowed as if to invite him over. Perhaps the buffalo wanted him to untie it. Perhaps it needed to urinate. He walked over and stood by the karuvelam thorn fence. He and the buffalo were surrounded by houses. He looked to see if he could spot any faces in the windows. There was only sun everywhere. The residents had shut themselves away from the heat. In the thousand metres he had walked, only one motorcycle had passed him. As it went by, he had pretended to wipe his face with his handkerchief so he couldn't be identified as an outsider.

He paced himself. He eyed the row houses. All five had curtains over their doors. He couldn't see which doors were open and which ones were closed. He didn't want to delay it too much. He walked casually down the row and quickly slid into the second house. She had left the door open. The moment he entered, he closed and bolted the door. He felt relieved. She was drawn from the kitchen by the sound. Her face was glowing. Laughing, she said, 'You've come, have you? And so early? I haven't got anything ready. I called you as soon as Akka left.' She went on and on, but he barely heard her.

He followed her to the kitchen. She was peeling baby onions. He slipped his arms around her waist and buried his face in her shoulder.

'Acting like a kattina purushan, with all the rights of a husband, are you? Let me go, da. Here, peel the onions for me,' she said, swatting his hands away. She laughed and slid out of his grasp, and he wore an exaggerated look of betrayal as he began to peel the onions.

'What, da, Purusha, are you angry?' she said.

'No, di, Pondaatti. Will my mission succeed if I get angry with you?' he laughed.

'What mission, Purusha?'

Every rejoinder made them laugh. They loved addressing each other as husband and wife. They kept it up.

Every time she called him 'Purusha', he wanted to plant a kiss on her face. Every time he called her 'Pondaatti', it felt as if the word had been invented just for her, that it bridged the gaps between them and came hurtling to her across all that kept them apart. They cooked together, chatting happily.

'Don't make too much, Pondaatti,' he said. It would eat up precious time. He caressed her every now and again.

'No one will return in a hurry, da, Purusha. Be patient, Purusha,' she laughed, pinching his cheeks. The pain from the pinch was the most pleasurable he had known. She was making drumstick kozhambu, which he loved, with potato curry. And payasam. She asked him to lay everything out in the hall, and began to make ulunduvadai. That was his favourite snack.

She saw him adjusting the tight trousers, which had begun to pinch his waist.

'I'll give you my father's lungi, da, Purusha,' she said and went to the bedroom. He followed her. There was a single bed in the small bedroom. The two cupboards had peacock motifs. She opened one and took out a lungi.

'You wear this and sit down, da, Purusha. I feel all sticky. I'll have a quick shower and come back, da, Purusha,' she said, opening the door.

She took five minutes to return. He stared at the door as he sat. She returned, her face flushed. The scent from her freshly showered body wafted through the house, subduing the smell of food. He followed her to the bedroom, held her close and said, 'You're killing me, di, Pondaatti.' He buried his face in her neck.

'Dei, Purusha…dei, Purusha,' she murmured, holding him tight and caressing his back.

'Adiyei, you whore! What are you doing?' came a scream.

The two of them turned in shock. Her akka

was standing outside the room, blocking all the light. Her face was in darkness, and her expression hidden. She stormed inside, grabbed her sister by the hair, and dragged her to the hall.

'You have the temerity to call him to our home, is it?' she said, and punched her hard on the back.

Looking at the spread, her akka kicked each vessel aside, spilling the contents everywhere. He didn't know what to do. For a moment, he wondered if he should run. But it wasn't right to leave her now.

Having kicked the food all over the floor, she returned to her sister and took aim.

He stepped between them. 'She's my pondaatti. You so much as raise your hand, and I'll kill you.'

'Oh, she's become your pondaatti, has she?' Her akka ground her teeth and slapped him.

He stood motionless, stunned. Her akka dragged her out from where she was cowering behind him.

'Purusha, Purusha,' she muttered, as her sister tugged at her arm. The word rose like a mantra, and she grabbed her akka's head and smashed it against the wall. Blood pouring down her face, her akka fell to the floor.

9

Kiss

Murugesu was waiting in his usual spot. It was a little thicket with a lallei tree at its centre. A bee sting bush had grown under the tree, covering most of it. Ivy gourd creepers climbed up the stalks. There were thorns at the bottom. The vegetation made a natural alcove, and he could camouflage the entrance by adjusting the limp stalks of the creeper. No one could make out the alcove or the man hidden inside. The alcove was spacious, quite like a cave. He had brought a rock inside, so he could sit on it and lean against the tree. As soon as he entered, he would poke at the rock, to make sure no dangerous reptile had crawled under it. Because he stopped by so frequently, it had acquired the warmth of a home. Perhaps, not too far in the future, it would be inviting enough to sleep in.

Once inside, he could go two or three hours without moving. Once he heard the much-anticipated sound of human speech, he would part the broad leaves of the bee sting bush so he could spy on the newcomers. His target was the neighbouring thicket, which had grown around a neem tree. Its branches spread out, forming a shelter as good as a camping tent. Once you were nestled inside, you could only see the sky from within.

From his own spot, he could hear the *mona-mona* of speech from the people climbing the steps to the hill temple, but couldn't make out the words. Couples looking for a cosy spot tended to find the neem thicket. They would make a beeline for it along the narrow path that broke off from the steps. Pimps and their clients knew the spot too. If someone like that happened to come along with a hooker, there was little point in staying, and he would end his vigil.

He entered the thicket around eleven that morning. When it was nearing noon and he still hadn't heard the murmur of speech, he wondered tiredly whether he would have to leave empty-handed that day. This could only go on till marriage. He had made up his mind not to so much as consider this pursuit once he was married.

He would reiterate this to himself every now and again. He didn't like sitting in the thicket, worried that a snake or lizard may lay claim to its share of his space. But there could be no easier way to go about his business. His ears perked up. Faraway sounds of speech seemed to float towards him. Were they the voices of lovers? How old would they be? He tried to discern this from the strains he heard.

His targets were young couples, particularly in the seventeen to twenty-two age group. They were the ones who were most reckless about their surroundings. The guilt they felt over doing something forbidden was greater too. They scared easily. They were so protective of each other that they would go so far as to sacrifice their lives for their lovers. And yet, if you threatened to take a picture of them together and upload it on the Internet, they would beg you not to. If they belonged to different castes, the despair in their pleas was exponentially greater.

Murugesu had only two props – a length of cloth that he wound around his face so only his eyes could be seen and a knife with a long, shiny blade. The knife was only to scare them. He hadn't drawn out a confrontation until it turned physical. He had simple demands. He would ask for their wallets and take away the money. If the boy wore a gold chain, he would take that too. He would ask the girl to hand over all her jewellery. Usually, they wore gold, a chain worth half a sovereign, earrings worth a quarter. That was all. People who could afford more than that did not sneak into places like this. Or perhaps people who sought places like this did not wear more gold than that.

He wouldn't touch his phone. He knew that could lead to problems. Once his work was done, he would chase them away and move to a different part of the hill, where he would rest under a flame of the forest tree. Then, he would saunter along the forest paths until he reached the road which led to the next village. There was a solitary bus stop there, where the town bus halted. He knew the timings. He would leave on that bus. Doing this once or twice a month supplemented his income nicely.

He worked as a salesman at a retail store in a town close to his village. He had to stand all day. On festival and auspicious days, a crowd milled around the counters. Although the shop didn't have too many customers on other days, the salespeople were not allowed to sit except when they had to sort new stock or paste stickers on them. Taking down clothes to spread them out for the customers and striking up banter with them to make a sale were the other tasks that made up his daily routine. His salary was just enough to keep himself afloat. It was a struggle to meet household expenses. And yet his family was on the lookout for a bride for him. He was running twenty-seven. His parents were determined to marry him off that year.

He spotted a couple climbing the stairs, just as he had expected. He couldn't see their faces clearly, but it was obvious to him that the lovers were young. They would stop here on their way back from the temple. He could see them look towards the neem tree as they went up. Yes, they would certainly return. They must come here frequently and think of it as their spot. He surveyed his surroundings. No one else had gone up the hill. The morning's faithful had already returned. He hoped nobody would show up before the lovers returned to their spot. Although he had been doing this for some time, it was hard to overcome the butterflies in his stomach before each encounter.

Murugesu had been involved in this line of work only for the past seven or eight months. It had all begun when he and his friends had come to the hill on a weekday. There were two ways up the hill – the steps and a pucca road. They went up the steps to the temple, prayed, and returned by the road. As they were rounding a corner, one of his friends happened to glance down the slope and caught sight of it. It was far away, but clear enough – under the tree, surrounded by thicket, lay a couple, limbs intertwined. The group watched silently for some time, but couldn't hold back when the boy began to undress his girlfriend.

'Dei! What do you think you're doing?' one of the friends yelled.

The couple jumped up in a hurry and looked in their direction, startled.

'What do you think you're doing right after visiting a temple?' another shouted, and that sent the couple scampering into the thicket.

By this time, a third member of their group had leapt down the slope and reached their hideout. He couldn't spot the couple. The lovers had another escape route. He came back with the girl's handbag and the boy's wallet, which they had left behind. The wallet held a little over a thousand rupees, and the handbag a hundred and fifty. They took the money out and tossed the wallet and purse by the side of the road.

'Poor things, da...they may not even have enough money for the bus,' one of the group said.

'People who behave like this deserve this, da. Let them walk,' another said.

'She looked like a very young girl,' said another.

'Perhaps, but she's got the guts to come here with him the moment he asks,' someone said contemptuously.

The money was spent blissfully at a TASMAC bar.

One of the friends laughed and said, 'If we do this once a month, that will take care of our TASMAC expenses!'

It was meant in a light vein, but took root in Murugesu's consciousness. It was that incident and his friend's words which had planted the seed for this plot of his. He had done his homework well. He'd visited the hill several times. The hill was about a mile's walk from the main road. It stood alone, surrounded by fields and pasture. It was a small hill – a child could run up the slope at one go – but the trees stood in thick clusters. Murugesu had found the forest path which led to the bus stop, so he wouldn't have to go back to the tar road with its shops. He'd made note of when there was a crowd, and when there were few visitors to the temple. He'd figured out the various spots that lovers had found on the hillside.

He did not have any accomplices. He took his time with the research before embarking on his ambushes. At first, he did what his friend had done – yelled at the couples to frighten and shame them. He might find a wallet or purse; at times, the couples had the presence of mind to run away with their belongings. It wasn't worth the time and trouble to return with nothing, and so he took it a step further. The knife was a useful addition to his kit, and worked well as a threat. The girls would get scared and move back. The boys tried to be heroes. But their girlfriends would calm them down. The girls were aware that the humiliation would be theirs alone if the matter got out.

As he had expected, the young couple returned to the thicket. She kept her handbag on the ground. The boy wasn't carrying anything. He must have his wallet in the back pocket of his trousers. Murugesu couldn't tell if the boy was wearing a chain from this distance. The lovers were laughing and talking, reaching out to each other every now and again.

This was the tricky part. He slipped out of his thicket and moved slowly towards their spot. The boy seemed to be persuading the girl to do something, and she was blushing and shaking her head. They were whispering together, and so he couldn't make out the words. Usually, the girls wore salwar kameez. This one was wearing a sari. Perhaps it was her birthday, or his. She looked beautiful in the sari. When the boy touched her cheek and turned her face to his, the sunlight accentuated the glow on that lovely face. Murugesu stopped to stare at them.

Suddenly she took the boy's face in her hands and pulled him in for a deep kiss. It appeared their lips were locked together. The boy didn't let go. They were frozen, eyes closed. Now, they would go further. But Murugesu didn't have the patience to wait. He felt things had gone far enough for his presence to scare them. He wound the cloth around his face and approached them noiselessly. They didn't hear him, oblivious as they were to the world, their lips interlocked.

He felt uncomfortable, and shouted, 'Dei, what do you think you're doing?'

The girl jumped at the sound of his voice, recoiled from her lover and stood up hurriedly. The boyfriend stood up too. They both looked about twenty, twenty-one. The boy wasn't wearing a chain. The chain around her neck was made of cheap metal – that would be of no use. She wore earrings too.

'Who are you, da?' the boy asked angrily. He was skinny, his stomach concave. But he was clearly furious – anyone would be if interrupted at such a moment, Murugesu thought.

Murugesu leapt towards the girl and grabbed her by the back of the head, gripping just above her loose plait. He placed the knife against her neck. 'Let me see those lips. Do you have honey on them? He was sucking on them like he would drink them up,' he said, turning her face towards him and staring at her lips. Her red lips, wet from the kiss, trembled. Murugesu felt an odd sensation.

'Dei, let her go…let her go, da!' the boy shouted, approaching Murugesu.

The girl held out a hand to say he shouldn't come any closer.

He stopped where he was and said, 'Let her go, da. What do you want, da?'

'Take out your wallet,' Murugesu said.

'I'm not carrying one.'

'How much money do you have?' Murugesu asked.

The boy felt in his shirt and trouser pockets and pulled out ten- and twenty-rupee notes. They made a total of about two hundred rupees.

'Chhi! Call yourself a man? You bring a girl here, with just two hundred rupees in your pocket? Aren't you ashamed?' Murugesu yelled, and hocked and spat at the boy. The boy hung his head.

He looked at the girl's ears. It was evident that her earrings were only gold-plated. The day's exertion had been pointless. He was looking at her, deflated, when a thought struck him. He decided to veer from his routine. Well, it would be the next leap in his line of work.

He asked the boy to take off his shirt. The boy obeyed hesitantly. His shirt and trousers were new, but inexpensive. He wasn't wearing a vest. He's come prepared, Murugesu thought. But there were no tan lines on his body. Perhaps he wasn't in the habit of wearing a vest. Murugesu hocked and spat at him again. The boy squirmed in embarrassment as Murugesu ran his eyes over his body.

'Where do you work, da?' Murugesu demanded.

The boy gave him the name of a large retail store in the state capital. So he was a kinsman. Murugesu felt rather sorry for him.

'Don't they sell vests in your shop?' he asked. Then he smirked. 'Are you wearing underpants at least? You've come all prepared, eh?'

He did not usually drag on the conversation to this extent. He had always felt dialogue should be kept to a minimum in this line of work. He was aware that he had overstepped his bounds.

He asked the boy to stand by the tree, and told the girl to bind his hands together behind him with his shirt, so his back was flat against the trunk. Her hair stayed in Murugesu's grasp, the knife remained at her neck. She stumbled her way through his orders. Murugesu tugged at the shirt to make sure she had tied the boy firmly. Then he asked her to take off her sari.

The moment she understood what he meant to do, she begged, 'Anna, please, no, anna...let me go, anna...' Her eyes were welling up, tears coursing down her cheeks.

'Take it off and tie his legs, di!' Murugesu commanded.

'Dei…let her go, da! Do whatever you want with me. But leave her alone!' The boy's voice had taken on a beseeching tone now.

'What can I do with you?' Murugesu snorted, and pressed the knife a little more firmly. With no option, she reached for her pallu. He loosened his grip just enough for her to move her hands.

She removed the pins with which she had fastened the pallu to her blouse, fingers slippery with sweat. He stared at her as she slowly unwound the sari. She had an attractive figure. It hit him that this would be the first body his flesh had known. And she was a beauty. He ached to hold her close. He would take her to his thicket. Would she come? Or would she shoot off some dialogue like, 'I'd rather die than…'? If he held the knife to the boy's neck, she would capitulate. Plans formed in his head within seconds.

Without entirely undoing her sari, she bent down to tie the boy's legs and turned her face to Murugesu's.

'Anna, let me go. Today's his birthday, anna. I wanted to give him a nice present, but I didn't have anything. I didn't have the money to buy him anything, anna. That's why I decided to give him something he's been asking of me for a long time – just one kiss. That's all, anna…I'm not that sort of girl, anna,' she said. She began to cry harder. 'Anna, this was our first kiss…I can still feel his lips on mine, anna…' She wept into her hands. He couldn't see her face. He could only hear her sobs.

Murugesu hesitated for a second, and then let go of her hair, pushing her aside.

'Go get lost!' he said and disappeared into the thicket.

AN EXTENSIVE LIBRARY

Including fresh, new, original Juggernaut books from the likes of Sunny Leone, Praveen Swami, Husain Haqqani, Umera Ahmed, Rujuta Diwekar and lots more. Plus, books from partner publishers and loads of free classics. Whichever genre you like, there's a book waiting for you.

CRUCIBLES OF SIN
HITESHA
Can a Geek ever find Love?
Finding Juliet
Toffee
Mary Shelley
Frankenstein
A FAROOQ RESHI INVESTIGATION
COLD FLAKE
PRAVEEN SWAMI
A Psychiatrist's Guide To Heartbreak
How to Heal Your Broken Heart
DR SHYAM BHAT
MOIN and THE MONSTER
ANUSHKA RAVISHANKAR
stories of women from the ganglands
S. Hussain Zaidi
with Jane Borges
Foreword by Vishal Bharadwaj
UMERA AHMED
Nowhere Girl
A Story of Love & Forgiveness
THE BEHEADING
This Is How He Will Bless Her
ABHEEK BARUA
THE Peshwa
The Lion and the Stallion
THE INVISIBLE WOMAN
SAURBH KATYAL
ANGRY BIRDS FAN? READ THE BOOK!
ANGRY BIRDS TOONS
TOONS TALES
ARCHANA SABOO
ADIKOOL
in
#AfricanAdventures
i am not a bimbette
Tarana Khan
She hates me. He loves me not but . . .
DON'T FALL IN LOVE
Vandana Shankar
KHUSHWANT SINGH
WE INDIANS

DON'T JUST READ; INTERACT

We're changing the reading experience from passive to active.

juggernaut.in

Ask authors questions

Get all your answers from the horse's mouth. Juggernaut authors actually reply to every question they can.

Rate and review

Let everyone know of your favourite reads or critique the finer points of a book – you will be heard in a community of like-minded readers.

Gift books to friends

For a book-lover, there's no nicer gift than a book personally picked. You can even do it anonymously if you like.

Enjoy new book formats

Discover serials released in parts over time, picture books including comics, and story-bundles at discounted rates. And coming soon, audiobooks.

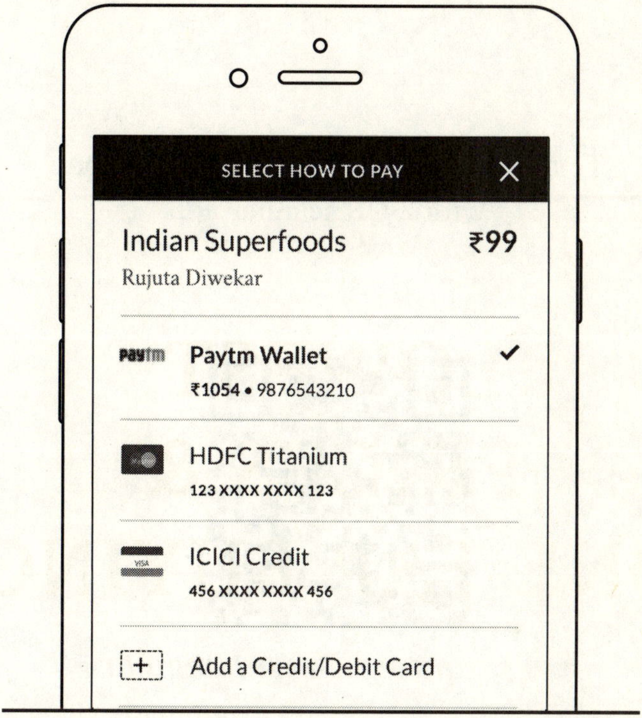
SELECT HOW TO PAY
Indian Superfoods
₹99
Rujuta Diwekar
Paytm Wallet
₹1054 • 9876543210
HDFC Titanium
123 XXXX XXXX 123
ICICI Credit
456 XXXX XXXX 456
Add a Credit/Debit Card

To download the app scan the QR Code with a QR scanner app